DIL DIES HARD

DIL DIES HARD

KELLY P. GAST

DOUBLEDAY & COMPANY, INC.
GARDEN CITY, NEW YORK
1975

All the characters in this book are fictitious, and any resemblance to actual persons, living or dead, is purely coincidental.

Library of Congress Cataloging in Publication Data
Gast, Kelly P
Dil dies hard.
I. Title.
PZ4.G25Di [PS3557.A847] 813'.5'4
ISBN 0-385-01513-5
Library of Congress Catalog Card Number 74-18799

Printed in the United States of America
First Edition

CHAPTER 1

After the first week Dil had gotten the knack of picking out a pine that was straight enough and free of limbs. The real trick was to pick one tall enough to be able to lop off a fence post or two after getting a standard-length telephone pole from the butt. He had been swinging a broad ax steadily for several hours when abruptly he noticed it: the jays and whiskey jacks were suddenly silent.

Dil had seen plenty of bear and cougar sign in the months since he had filed for this section. He glanced at his venerable 45-90 and made sure it was within reach. He paused for a moment, then realized that whatever had silenced the birds must have been listening to the whack of his ax. He went back to limbing a pole. It was late October and the half minute he had stopped working was enough to make him shiver at this altitude. "Some varmint," he told himself.

But he could not shake off the feel that something big was watching him. A hundred yards away his team grazed, bridles off but still in double harness. Their ears pointed downhill. Dil checked his 45-90 again. It was an ancient piece, heavy and not particularly accurate. But it was the only thing that had ever come back out of Alaska after his father had gone chasing off after gold with all the other damn fools who died or disappeared somewhere on the wrong side of Chilkoot Pass. And in 1915 money wasn't so plentiful that Dil could splurge on a newer rifle.

Then he suddenly saw the solution to his winter meat problem. Even for this virgin country the elk was a giant.

A bull—which meant the meat would be strong, but Dil had eaten worse. As he raised his rifle he calculated that this one ought to dress out a good three hundred.

Then just as abruptly Dil lowered the rifle. Those jays and whiskey jacks would not have fallen silent even for the most magnificent elk on earth. Something else was prowling these woods. And Dil knew with a sudden gut certainty just what it was.

"Just mind you watch out for that Groby," the merchant who sold him ammunition had warned.

"Who?"

"Groby. Humdinger calls himself a game warden."

"What's that?"

The hardware merchant had shrugged. "Goldang guvmint just thunk up another new way t'keep a farmer from gittin' rid of every kind of crop-eatin' varmint. But mind you, don't let him catch you with any meat or you'll end up in jail."

Dil watched the bull elk's magnificent and leisurely progression toward the clearing where his team grazed. The horses eyed the elk for a moment, then returned to their munching. Dil sighed and put down his rifle. Somewhere, he knew, somebody was watching. Probably Groby.

He was just picking up his ax again when he heard a whining *whirrrrrrr* and an instant later the flat *whap* of a carbine. Unbelieving, he saw bark fly from the pole he had been limbing. Now he knew what had quieted the whiskey jacks. It had to be a city hunter.

Dil scooted down behind the mound of brush he had trimmed and gave his horses an anxious glance. The city-headed hunter hadn't hit them so far. "You stop that crazy shootin'," Dil yelled, "or I'll put a round up your pants leg!"

In reply another bullet whirred through the pile of brush where he was trying to hide. Dil scooted around, trying to lie flat behind the pole. Ax and rifle were only a yard away. He wondered who was shooting at him. Groby? He had never met the man so it didn't seem likely. He glanced back toward his horses. The bull elk was long gone but his team munched the fall grass, oblivious of the shooting. Gradually it soaked into Dil that this was not an accident. The first shot had been a near miss. So had the second. A tiny, tickling trickle ran between his shoulder blades as he realized that he was not dealing with a trigger-happy city hunter. Somebody out there was trying to kill him!

Dil didn't mind admitting he was scared. Nobody had ever—well, if you counted rocksalt-loaded shotguns and watermelon patches . . . But he was twenty-three now, past the age of childish pranks. He searched his memory. Even where he had grown up and people knew him he couldn't think of anybody who had reason to kill him. And here . . .

He had been in this country only since the spring thaw. Apart from the hardware man and the grocer the only person he knew was the telephone company agent who bought his fresh-cut poles whenever he hitched up the team for the sixteen miles of mud and axle-bursting road into town. He supposed he must have met other people when he rode into the county seat and searched out the courthouse to file on this section. But he couldn't remember.

Anyhow, with somebody shooting at him, it was no time to examine his conscience. He scrabbled around in the mass of brush and fallen needles, looking for a rock. Finally he settled for a pine cone. He thought for an instant, calculating the direction from which the bullets had come. Then, with as much force as he could muster lying prone, he threw the pine cone to one side. It fell in a thicket and instantly there came another shot.

But by now Dil had his rifle. He checked and made sure

that it was loaded. His jacket was hanging ten feet away, with another half-dozen rounds in the pocket. He guessed it didn't make any real difference.

Down in the meadow the horses were becoming nervous. Irrationally Dil prayed they wouldn't panic and tear up the harness. He knew better than to try to work his way toward them. His team were Canadian Chunks, good for pulling but no great shakes for riding even if they hadn't been hitched together. He wondered if whoever was shooting at him wanted the horses. He couldn't think of anything else he owned that would be worth killing a man for. Goldang! What kind of country had he picked to settle in?

Somewhere uphill a crow cawed. Dil turned his head carefully. He saw nothing. He had his rifle now. But so did the other man. He peered about, looking for an escape route. The hillside was still forested, dotted here and there by brush piles where he had felled and limbed a pole. Come snow he would burn the brush piles, but . . . how was he going to get out of here?

Whoever it was had panicked and snapped a shot at the tossed pine cone. He would not make the same mistake twice. And Dil was still pinned down where the man had gotten two shots at him. He gazed upward where the sunlight filtered through a mixed stand of lodgepole and spruce. It still lacked at least an hour of dark. Dil shivered and wished that he had his jacket. Ten feet. Those ten feet could cost him his life and he had a half dozen more rounds in his jacket pocket. It was growing chilly and he was reminded of the land office man's description of the country he had decided to homestead.

"Bear Creek?" the bewhiskered man had laughed. "Wha', they ain't nothin' there but cougars and varmints. And the climate–hell, you got nine months' winter and t'other three're damn late in the fall."

But abruptly Dil realized that there must be something else here besides poles and polecats. Otherwise, why was somebody trying to get him off this section?

The crow cawed again and this time Dil sensed which direction the menace came from. It was downhill and quite a ways from where he had thought it was. Then as he stared unbelieving the man stood, exposing himself carelessly as he walked toward Dil's horses. Abruptly Dil realized what this meant. *He doesn't know I've got a rifle.*

The man was moving easily and purposefully, not even glancing around. Dil studied him. The man was big and seemed even bigger because of the bay-blanket coat he wore. Graying red hair straggled from the edges of his stocking cap. His face was concealed beneath a half-inch growth of graying red beard.

Dil searched his memory. He guessed he'd probably seen the stranger somewhere in town but he couldn't remember ever crossing him. While the stranger walked toward the horses, carrying his carbine in his left hand, Dil silently got to his feet. He thought about grabbing his coat and the cartridges but if he waited another second the stranger would have his horses and then Dil would be afoot, three miles from his lean-to and thirteen from the nearest town.

Dil had hunted enough to know better than to run. He had to keep cool, not lose his breath and start panting until he couldn't hit the hornless end of a bull with a scoop shovel. He forced himself to take deep breaths. Slowly he got to his feet and began stalking toward the meadow.

His harnessed Chunks glanced hopefully at the stranger. When there was no sugar-in-my-hand gesture they moseyed on and began cropping grass just out of reach. Dil was still a hundred yards away. He marveled at the stranger's arrogance, then realized that this giant of a man must have become used to scaring people to death with a glance. Probably he assumed that Dil had lit running after the second shot and was well over the mountain by now. Looking at the stranger's calm assurance, Dil wished he were.

The stranger was sweet-talking the horses now, trying to get within reach. If he hadn't been so scared Dil would have laughed at the way the horses stepped off in unison, trotting easily about the meadow without once putting a strain on the harness which bound them together.

Silently Dil moved downhill. He had covered half the distance before the horses noticed him and pointed their ears. Immediately the big stranger wheeled and fired without even shouldering his carbine. The shot went wide. The horses snorted and trotted in the other direction. Somewhere uphill the crow cawed again.

Dil fell forward instinctively as the other man fired. Halfway down he realized that the hillside was steeper than he had thought and he was going to land harder than he had planned. The 45-90 clattered but did not go off. He lay numbed for a moment, not breathless but dazed from the jolt. The stranger levered another round into his carbine and snapped off another shot. He missed again.

Dil slid downhill on his belly until he could reach his rifle. He fumbled with safety and hammer and finally convinced himself that it was ready to fire. It was awkward to aim from this position, with his head lower than his feet. He braced himself and held his breath, willing himself not to tremble. Half of his mind remembered old wives' tales about a drowning man's life flashing before him. Dil didn't reconstruct any childhood memories. He only hoped he hadn't damaged his father's old rifle in the fall.

He teetered on his elbows, twisting his spine to aim at the giant in the bay-blanket coat. From the far side of the meadow the horses wheeled in unison to stand and watch. The big stranger was levering a third shot into the magazine. Dil knew that sooner or later one of those shots was going to connect. He could feel his elbows trembling from the strain of this strange position. He wished there were time, or a log, anything to rest this heavy weapon on. The man was blurring in the sights as he strained to hold a bead.

Dil winked and a tear streamed down his cheek. Son of a gun, couldn't he hold still for a minute! He pulled the trigger and nothing happened. *Misfire!* Then he knew he hadn't heard the hammer click. Hadn't even cocked it! Everything seemed to be moving in slow motion, like it had in that nickelodeon he had seen one day in town. The big man was still jacking his third shell into the magazine when Dil finally jerked the hammer until it clicked twice.

He drew another breath and held it, wondering if the water in his eyes was sweat or tears. He saw the front sight waving wildly back and forth across the man in the bay-blanket jacket. The big man had finally levered his bullet into the chamber. He was going to shoulder the carbine this time.

Dil began squeezing the trigger. The barrel of his 45-90 still waved crazily. At one instant he saw his off mare gazing reproachfully at him over the front sight. Then it swung back to sweep past the man who had shot at him. He squeezed a little more.

The rifle went off before he had expected it to. The other man shot at the same instant and Dil heard—*felt*—the bullet's passage over his head. He prayed for the strength to get another cartridge into the chamber before the big man could reload. The recoil had jolted the bejesus out of him in this cramped position. He felt numb all over and for a moment wondered if he had been shot.

Muttering and mumbling, he managed to get the old rifle loaded and cocked again. Then he realized that the other man was not reloading. The stranger was glaring at him with a hatred that Dil could not remember having done anything to deserve. His teeth bared in a snarl. Then he dropped the carbine. A moment later he knelt to pick it up. Then he fell flat on his face, atop the gun. From across the meadow the harnessed team stared, ears pointing forward.

"A lot of help you were," Dil grunted. He struggled to his feet, his cocked rifle pointing at the other man. He walked toward him, looking for some tensing of muscle that would mean the stranger was playing possum. The stranger didn't move.

Dil prodded him with his rifle barrel. There was no response. With his boot he managed to shift the inert, bay-blanketed body until it faced upward. Eyes stared. Dil stared back. Only when a deer fly settled on one of the staring pupils did Dil really believe that he had killed a stranger.

CHAPTER 2

When he finally realized that he had killed a man Dil's stomach was the first part of him to react. It was a long time before he stopped shivering and could force his watery eyes to focus again. When they did the dead man was still there, his huge body wrapped irrevocably around one of Dil's bullets.

Dil was shivering. In another hour it would be dark. He poked the stiffening body again, still unwilling to believe that the stranger was dead. Then he went back uphill and got his coat. What, he wondered, was he going to do now. He wondered who the stranger was—how many friends or family he had. Dil was suddenly and acutely aware of his own status in Bear Creek. He had been here a couple of months, had no family and fewer friends.

Maybe he ought to just dig a hole and bury the stranger. It would be simplest. But . . . how did he know the stranger had been alone? No matter what he did, Dil suspected that it would be the wrong thing. But hell, he told himself, this was 1915. They didn't have posses and lynch mobs anymore. The West was all settled now, roads, automobiles, even telephones!

He studied the stranger again. Reddish-gray hair and a half inch of beard. A huge man. Remembering the contemptuous way this man had walked down to the meadow to catch his horses, Dil guessed that this man must have been used to getting his own way. He supposed he ought to go through the stranger's pockets and learn what he could. But he couldn't bring himself to do it.

Instead Dil clucked at his team until the Chunks stood still long enough for him to get their bits back in. He could see no blood about the corpse—didn't even know where he had hit it, but he supposed the horses would smell it. He tested the wind and circled the team around the meadow to approach the body from the proper direction.

It was even heavier than he had expected. Finally he put a length of line about the stranger's ankles and passed it over Nellie's back, then under her belly, where he could snub it. Little by little he got the burden atop the mare, where he could secure it with a diamond hitch. He was climbing atop Bill when suddenly he changed his mind.

He had a load of poles nearly cut. It was less than an hour till dark. To hell with stumbling along in the dark and maybe breaking a horse's leg! He fastened a length of rope to the corpse's ankles, passed it through the fork of a lightning-struck tamarack, and unhitched Bill. Moments later the body hung by the heels but up safe from predators. He got back on Bill and led Nellie the couple of miles back to the lean-to.

It would be better, he knew, to let the horses pasture in the meadow but it was only mid-October and the bear were still out. Besides, he never knew when a hungry cougar would turn up in this country. Bill and Nellie stared so reproachfully at him from the edge of the firelight that he surrendered and gave them each a biscuit. Somehow he had to get together poles enough to enclose the last side of his lean-to. And that meant that somehow he had to scrape together money for a stove and a few lengths of stovepipe. He curled up in his blankets, staring into the dying fire, trying not to think about what hung by its heels in the clearing.

Might as well will himself not to think about purple

giraffes. He turned it over in his mind, trying to find some innocent explanation. There was none. There could be no grounds for misunderstanding when a stranger had bushwhacked him, putting two shots near him before he even knew he was a target. If it had been some city hunter's stupidity the man could have made himself scarce instead of provoking a showdown. There was no talking himself out of it. This stranger had tried to kill him. Why?

Dil was no angel but he couldn't remember ever doing anybody the kind of dirt that would bring this much of a grudge. Most of his life had been spent drudging away at any job he could find to keep his mother and his kid brother alive after Papa had gone off to the Klondike and never come back. Now Mama had given up the struggle and gone to join Papa, wherever that might be, and his kid brother had gone off to see the world through a porthole. At twenty-three Dil thought it was time he started looking out for his own future.

But, like most people, he had been born thirty years too soon or too late, depending on whose viewpoint. The good land had all been homesteaded and foreclosed by banks and railroads long ago. When the government had opened this area for filing nobody in his right mind had been willing to go sixteen miles over an unpaved road to claim 640 acres of scrub-timbered hillside. Nobody except Dil and a few other optimists who had nothing better to do.

If he ever got all the poles logged off he could plant a garden. Maybe even a few acres of rye or barley in the meadow. The season at this altitude was too short for wheat. But if he could just cut enough hay to get Bill and Nellie through the winter, who knew . . . maybe next year he could even get a cow! And with a cow, why, maybe someday he might even dare to think about acquiring a wife!

But first he had to get rid of that big thing hanging by

its heels in the meadow. Who the hell was he? Maybe it would be better just to bury him or leave him for the coyotes to scatter. If the man had not been alone something should have happened by now. Either somebody would be out here with the sheriff or a bullet would have found Dil as he had crouched outlined by his campfire this evening.

Nellie whinnied. Somewhere in the distance an owl hooted. Dil burrowed deeper into his blankets and tried to imagine how snug it would be once he got another wall built onto this lean-to and a stove working. Once it froze he would get around to splitting the butts and trimmings from his pole cutting—once he got runners fitted to the wagon.

When he awakened, Bill and Nellie stood over him, waiting for him to drive them back to pasture. He yawned his way through morning chores, deliberately turning his mind off of what lay ahead. Finally he could put it off no longer. He harnessed the Chunks to the pole wagon and trotted them the two miles to the meadow.

The thing hanging by its feet was even less attractive than it had been yesterday but at least the varmints hadn't been eating at it. He levered and pried until he had his poles loaded, then ran the wagon under the tree. The body was still stiff. He didn't know much about things like rigor mortis but he suspected that it was just frozen. Finally he worked it around lengthwise until it lay like another pole atop the load. He tied a piece of canvas over it and clucked until Bill and Nellie were trotting the remaining fourteen miles into town.

It was nearing noon before he trotted down the dusty main street of Winville. Pulling up in front of the sheriff's office, he was sorry he'd brought the body into town. The stranger must have been working alone. Should have left well enough alone, he told himself. But it was too late now. Kids who had been climbing over the shiny Model T roadster in front of the sheriff's office were already getting curious about what he had under the canvas. Dil tied his team and went inside.

He had never met the sheriff of this county and Dil suddenly realized that he had been expecting something quite different from the scholarly-looking little man in pince-nez and a sheepskin vest who sat reading yesterday's *Spokesman Review*. Dil stared, wondering how to tell it. Finally he just told the truth.

The sheriff studied him with expressionless eyes. "You got him on your wagon?" he finally asked.

Dil nodded.

They went outside together. The sheriff shooed the boys away before peeking under a corner of the canvas. Then, turning to one of the older boys, he called, "Go get Doc Goetter."

There was more brouhaha getting the corpse off the wagon and into a funeral parlor. Meanwhile it was getting later in the afternoon and Dil guessed that he was going to be out the cost of a meal for his horses. He was wondering how much the livery stable would demand out of the proceeds of his poles when he abruptly realized that the sheriff was talking to him again. "Huh?" he asked.

"You're sure you don't know him?"

"Nope," Dil said. "Never laid eyes on him before yesterday."

"Then why'd you kill him?"

Dil shrugged. "It was him or me. And seein's he was on my land, shootin' at me, makin' to steal my horses . . ." He left it dangling.

The sheriff's eyes were still noncommittal. "Why don't you start over at the beginning?" he asked.

"I got to unload my poles and get some hay into my horses," Dil protested.

"Relax," the sheriff said. "If you're telling the truth it won't take long."

"Could you tell me something first?" Dil asked. "Who is he?"

"Jake Nelson," the sheriff said. "He proved up on the section downstream from you some five years ago."

Dil waited.

"Doesn't that mean anything to you?" the sheriff asked.

"Should it?"

The sheriff shrugged. "Maybe he got the idea you were fixin' to dam up his water."

Dil said nothing.

The sheriff shrugged again. "Old Jake wasn't the easiest neighbor to get along with," he said.

Finally it was over and Dil was free to sell his poles to the telephone company agent. He stopped at the Mercantile and bought flour, salt, soda, and soap. After the clerk had totaled the bill he considered for a moment, then added a pound of coffee. Outside he studied the sun. If he were to trot Bill and Nellie the first couple of miles there would be some graze where they could refuel for the long uphill walk back to the lean-to. He clucked the team into motion.

He still didn't understand what had happened. The sheriff had been purposely vague, offering no unnecessary comment apart from his farewell, "Don't start making a habit of it." Bouncing along on the front truck of the pole wagon, Dil wondered what kind of a man he had killed. Surely he must have had some standing—some friends or enemies in the community. It all seemed so odd, so purposeless. A man had tried to kill him. He had shot back and killed the man. And was that all there was to it?

The sheriff had gone through his story several times and seemed satisfied that he was telling the truth. He wondered if there would be further inquiries. Vaguely he remembered something about coroner's juries or some such thing. It seemed somehow indecent that a killing caused so little flutter in this tiny town. He shivered at the realization that it might have caused even less flutter if it had been the other way around, with himself, Dil, the stranger and victim instead of Jake Nelson. He wondered if the townspeople were callous and unfeeling. Maybe they were actually happy to see the last of Jake Nelson.

To hell with it. He slapped the reins over old Bill's rump until he had pulled his side of the doubletree up even with Nellie's. They trotted with the afternoon sun on their backs until he reached the ford where there was still a fair amount of pasture.

The team crossed the ford, puffing and splashing as they dragged the wagon through the knee-high water. Finally they topped the opposite bank and, without his reining them in, both horses stopped. Dil got off the front truck and took off their bridles. Then, while the pair of Chunks was grazing, he undid the tugs and tongue straps. The horses neighed and meandered off into thicker grass.

Dil wandered about the wagon, checking for loose parts. If he didn't get a bear soon he was going to have to buy some axle grease. And if he didn't get some fat meat soon he was going to be in one hell of a shape for the winter. He lay on the grass, soaking up the last of the afternoon sun and wishing that he had been able to afford some crackers or something. Bill and Nellie were filling up all right but it was going to be a right smart trot before Dil was back to the lean-to, where he could convert the flour into biscuits.

He thought about Jake Nelson, who had tried to kill him. Then he thought about how long his flour would last, whether he would be able to finish the last wall of the lean-to and maybe put in a mud-lined hearth until he could afford a stove. If he could just hold out a couple of weeks before he was starved into cutting another load of poles . . .

Son of a gun! If only he'd had a pencil and some paper he might have made a list. Now he knew what he needed and what he had forgotten. The scythe was so dull that he had practically given up haymaking. He needed a whetstone. He studied the sun and the distance back into town. Maybe he could ride one of the horses back in. But . . .

They were stupid beasts but they were all he had and if he didn't take care of them he would have nothing. Better let them fill up on grass while they could. It was still fourteen miles to the lean-to.

Judas Priest, would the Mercantile still be open by the time he could hoof it back in to town? He didn't know. To hell with it, he decided. Once he got back to the lean-to he could paw through the creek bottom until he found a stone that would do to put an edge on the scythe. All it took was time. If only there were a few more hours of daylight . . .

He sighed and rose to his feet. The horses were still packing it away but he guessed they'd had enough to make it home. He was just easing toward them with the bridles when he abruptly learned that the business of Jake Nelson was not finished yet. A shot rang out and Nellie collapsed. There was a tiny red hole in the white patch on her forehead.

CHAPTER 3

Dil stood unbelieving for a moment, then fell flat in the short grass. He looked up the creek in the direction whence came the shot. Solid buckbrush that would give pause even to a bullsnake. And somewhere behind that cover was a man with a rifle.

Dil's 45-90 was back in the lean-to. Stupid, he guessed. But what kind of a country was it where a man had to bring a gun to town? In the country where Dil had grown up everybody had firearms. But they were for varmints or for knocking over meat. Judas Priest, he thought, first me, then my horse! What kind of polecats lived around here?

He waited for the next shot to drop old Bill. It never came. After he had cowered for a quarter of an hour in the grass he finally raised his head cautiously. Old Bill, after one sniff at Nellie, had gone back to cropping grass. Though he didn't have the words to formulate it properly, Dil wondered if this was what life had been like before Eve and her apple—the ability to live blissfully in an eternal present with no thought for past or future.

He couldn't sit here all night and freeze to death. It was starting to get dark. He eased up to Bill, slipped the bridle onto him, and mounted; then, bending low over the Chunk's neck, expecting a bullet at any moment, he dug in his heels and kicked until the old horse broke into a lumbering gallop.

When he got back to town the sheriff's office was locked and dark. He glanced down the street. The Mercantile was dark too. That left only the Jim Hill Hotel. He found the tiny sheriff polishing off a man-sized portion of liver and onions.

"This time they got my horse down by the ford," Dil said.

The sheriff put down his coffee cup. "You sure you got no idea who?" he asked.

"I'm a stranger here," Dil protested. "I only been in this country a couple of months. I been too busy gettin' set for winter to make any enemies."

The sheriff shrugged. "Well," he said, "I'm sorry 'bout your horse but there isn't much I can do."

"Can't you do nothin'?"

The sheriff shrugged again. "Me'n one deputy are all the law in this country. And this county's a hundred miles square, most of it mountains and one side bordering the reservation. You tell me who's doin' you dirty and I'll go out and get him."

"It's got to be some friend or relation of that, uh—Jake Nelson."

"Sounds reasonable," the sheriff said as he slurped more coffee. "You know who?"

"No."

"Neither do I. Jake Nelson never had no truck with nobody."

So there it stood after considerable wrangling and repetition on both sides, and now Dil was riding home in the dark, carrying his groceries in front of him on old Bill's broad back.

Tomorrow he would have to see about getting the wagon back home before some of these no-goods stole it too. Somewhere he heard an owl hoot. Hair rose on the back of his neck as he wondered if it was a real owl. If he ever got home to the lean-to—and if somebody hadn't gotten there first—he solemnly resolved never to be separated from his 45-90 again. The Winchester was an obsolete relic but it had killed one man. He hoped it would last long enough to kill another. Remembering how Nellie had lain on her side in the grass with a late October fly buzzing around the hole in her forehead, he gritted his teeth and almost forgot how frightened he was.

Old Bill stumbled and Dil struggled not to lose his groceries or fall off the horse's broad, bare back. He wished he could be like a cowboy he had read about once in a dime novel—a two-gun man with a silver-mounted saddle who was afraid of nothing. Instead he had half of a team of Canadian Chunks, good, hard-working horses but only slightly more suitable for riding than a Clydesdale or Percheron. And if he didn't get back to where he had hidden his rifle near the lean-to he might not even have one gun, much less two. He wondered if cowboys ever lived like they did in the dime novels, riding madly about the country rescuing rich men's daughters and killing villains by the dozen.

Finally, several eternities later, he was home, and so exhausted from the ride to and from town that he went to bed too tired to remedy the hunger that had nearly driven him mad when he'd reported the killing of his horse to the supping sheriff.

With morning he felt slightly better. After biscuits he cleaned the 45-90 and checked his ammunition. He had nineteen rounds. It might see him through the winter if he didn't have to waste it all in some fool feud he didn't even understand.

"What the hell am I going to do?" he asked.

Old Bill was sympathetic but offered no solution. There was no use trying to haul more poles with only one horse. He hitched up Bill and went off uphill to cut thinner lodgepoles and close off the open side of his lean-to. He still didn't know how he was going to rig a fireplace that wouldn't burn the place down. All morning as he cut and dragged poles he tried to figure it out. There was a way of plastering clay onto logs and making a fireplace but even if he had known how to do it there wasn't any clay this high up in the mountains. Then suddenly around noon he thought of the solution.

Technically, he guessed, it was stealing, but . . . for no good reason Jake Nelson had tried to take his life. If he could find the dead man's cabin he guessed he would be justified in appropriating a stove. If Jake Nelson was where Dil hoped he was he would already be warm enough. He put the bridle on Bill, checked his 45-90 again, and began riding bareback down the dirt road to town.

He had always assumed that there were neighbors somewhere along this road but what with the rush of trying to get settled in before the first snow Dil had never gone out of his way to look for them. He rode slowly, letting old Bill take his head. The twin ruts followed the creek for a couple of miles, then struck off across a flat of jackpines with a ten-yard pothole in the center. As he passed the pothole a loon shrieked like the Kaiser at Verdun and went flapping away through the pines. A quarter mile farther Dil saw the faint path branching off from the ruts.

"Hey, mister!"

Dil spun on old Bill's broad, bare back and saw a teenage kid in bib overalls and floppy straw hat. Belatedly he realized that he was pointing his rifle at the stranger. "Sorry," he mumbled, and turned the octagonal-barreled relic in the opposite direction.

"Mister, you seen a stray cow anywhere around here?"

Dil hadn't and said so. He was about to ride on when he realized that it would be just as well not to be seen heading down the path toward the shanty of the man he had just killed. Suddenly he realized that Jake Nelson might have had stock or chickens penned up that would need watering by now.

"You're new around here, ain't you?"

"Yup," Dil said. He wished the kid would go off and look for his cow.

"I'm Hallie Haines," the kid in the floppy hat said. "My folks live a piece down the road."

Dil was about to remark that Hallie was a funny name for a boy when he noticed an incipient something behind the bib of her overalls. He pulled off his hat, freeing a shock of uncontrollable red hair, and muttered, "Pleased t'meetcha. I'm Dil Reeves."

They looked at each other in silent surmise, neither quite knowing what to say next. "Well," Hallie finally managed, "I got to go find that dang cow."

"Yup," Dil said. If she was going to use that kind of language he didn't know why he had bothered to take off his hat. They edged their horses past each other and moved apart.

A hundred yards farther he heard her yell, "Dil?"

"Yup?"

"You get caught up on your work, you come over and set a spell."

"I will," Dil promised. He kept riding until he judged that she had gotten out of sight, then doubled back and began picking his way down the barely visible track that led, he supposed, to Jake Nelson's.

From what little he had been able to glean from the uncommunicative sheriff, Jake Nelson had been a bachelor, a misanthrope, a hermit who was not overly delicate on the difference between mine and thine. Though the little man had not exactly come out and said it, Dil had received the general impression that the solitary giant's demise had been regarded as good riddance. Still, he felt a little queer about looting the dead man's effects.

Thinking it over, he guessed that what made him much more nervous was the knowledge that Nellie had been shot well after Jake Nelson was stiff and cold. He checked the action on the 45-90 again. His neck and shoulder were still sore from firing it in an awkward position. He hoped he wouldn't have to shoot again.

Jake Nelson's cabin was back on the creek again, several miles downstream from Dil's lean-to. There was a pole corral behind the cabin and a log-and-moss-chinked stable. Dil looked in. There were horse droppings but no cow sign. The stable needed forking out but . . .

Puzzled, Dil squatted in the stable. There was a licked and chewed oat box in the bottom of the manger. The stable stank of manure and horses but Dil's practiced nose told him that there had been no horse in here for at least a fortnight. He went out again and walked to where old Bill was cropping weeds by the cabin.

The latch string was not hanging out but it took Dil only a second to lift the bar with the blade of his jackknife. Inside the cabin was permeated with the inimitable sweet-gamy stink that develops over the years around a dirty old man too busy or too lazy for housework. In one corner of the cabin was a knee-high stack of blankets. Looted, Dil guessed by their infinite variety, from bindle stiffs who had crossed the jolly giant's path and lost the last of their worldly possessions. In the opposite corner was a square-topped, four-lidded laundry stove with the grate only half burned out. The stovepipe was practically new.

Atop the stove was a greasy skillet with meat-flecked fat in it, peppered with mouse and rat turds. Beside the skillet was a cast-iron bowl half filled with soured and drying oatmeal. Dil glanced outside again. Jays and whiskey jacks had become inured to old Bill's presence and were shrieking as they crisscrossed the tiny clearing. Dil went back in and began taking apart the stove.

He had it loaded on old Bill in two more or less equal portions, padded with a few blankets from the stack, and was just ready to leave when he heard the labored grinding of a Model T struggling up the rutted Bear Creek road.

Durn! Dil thought. That'll be the sheriff. He guessed that he could get away through the slash pine and buck-brush without being seen. But . . . to hell with it. If the sheriff couldn't control this county any better than he was doing. . . . Dil decided to brazen it out. After what Jake Nelson had tried to do to him, Dil felt he was owed a stove. He began leading Bill out to the road.

To his surprise the Ford went right on by before he got in sight of the road. Must be headin' out to my place, Dil guessed. He led Bill out to the twin ruts and they began walking back uphill. It was nearing noon and Dil could feel the biscuits wearing thin. He caught himself wondering about the girl out hunting the stray cow. She hadn't exactly thrown rocks at him. He wondered if somehow he could swing the loan of a horse maybe from her pa and go salvage his wagon—maybe even haul a few more loads of poles and lay in a couple of sacks of macaroni and beans for the cold months. Then he heard the Ford laboring back toward him.

Once more Dil was tempted to duck into the brush and let the sheriff go on by. But that would only be putting it off. If the sheriff had come out here to look over Jake Nelson's property he would have known where to turn off. Since he hadn't, the little man had to have made this trip to see Dil. Maybe he had changed his mind and decided to arrest him. Dil wished he knew somebody around here. Maybe he should have spent less time working and a little more getting acquainted with his neighbors.

The Ford was mired in a muddy spot next to the pothole where Dil had flushed a loon. Two men in four-cornered engineer's hats pushed while a third played delicately with low and reverse pedals, struggling to rock the high-centered flivver out of the hole. Dil halted at the edge of the clearing. It was not the sheriff's roadster. This was a black touring car with top and windshield down. The three men in the car saw Dil and his horse. The engine stopped and the radiator began spouting steam.

"Hey, rube," one of the men called. "You want to make four bits?"

Dil moved toward the three men, wondering what they were up to this far from town. There was a transit in the back of the flivver and the men looked like a railroad survey crew. But Dil knew there wasn't the chance of a snowball in hell of ever seeing a railroad on Bear Creek. The country was too steep. Besides, it didn't go anywhere.

"You want to make four bits?" one of the men repeated.

Dil had been going to offer them a tow out of simple neighborliness but he didn't take kindly to being called a rube. "Don't know if I do," he said. "Seems t'me you're in at least a dollar's worth."

Two of the men laughed. The one who had called Dil a rube glowered and muttered something but after a moment's internal struggle he produced a silver dollar. Dil pocketed it and passed a lariat from old Bill to the front axle of the flivver. In a moment he had the car out of the mud.

"By the way," one of the men asked, "where you going with Jake Nelson's stove?"

CHAPTER 4

A sudden scare shot through Dil. His hands whitened over the stock of the 45-90 as he faced the three men. Then he realized that nobody had drawn on him. "Nelson didn't need it anymore," he said in a flat voice. "I figured he owed it to me."

The three men in engineer's hats stared at him. Dil stared back. "Somebody owes me a horse too," Dil finally added. "You got any idea who that might be?" Something had happened to his voice. The words came out flat and grating.

The three strangers looked at each other in consternation. "Thanks for the tow, rube," one said. Hastily they cranked life back into the steaming flivver and went bouncing down the road toward town.

Dil was ashamed. He knew he ought not to have acted that way with strangers who probably had no connection with his problems. Then he remembered what had started it. One of them had known Jake Nelson well enough to recognize his stove. What were they doing poking around here in Bear Creek anyway? If he'd been a little less hairtrigger with his answers he might have been able to pump some information from them.

Well, hell, he guessed that he had a right to be nervous. But as he plodded uphill, leading old Bill, he knew what was wrong. Owed him or not, he just hadn't felt right about looting a dead man's cabin. He studied the sun. With luck he could be back at the lean-to in time to get in a couple of hours' work before dark. If something didn't happen first. He knew that whoever had shot Nellie wasn't going to leave it at that. And what had those three dudes in the funny hats been up to out here on this road? His ruminations were cut short by the sound of a cow. From the continuous bleating moan it sounded like she was bulling.

Immediately he remembered the scrawny girl in the bib overalls and the look that had passed between them. It occurred to him to wonder for a moment if Hallie Haines had been bulling too. Probably there weren't too many young men homesteading on Bear Creek. But he put aside such dangerous thoughts as he led old Bill uphill toward the sound of the bawling heifer.

She had tangled her lead rope in a clump of sumac less than a mile from his lean-to. The heifer's udder was swollen and sore. He wished he had a bucket or pan of some kind but not even his hat would serve. Sighing, he got her rope from around the gnarled sumac trunks and tied it to old Bill's halter. The end of the rope was not frayed or broken. It looked like a fresh cut.

He passed a muddy spot in the twin ruts which county maps jestingly referred to as a road and saw imprinted the diamond-back pattern of the flivver's 30-inch-by-3-inch clincher tires. But when he reached his lean-to he could see no signs of prowling. He got the stove off Bill and hobbled him, then emptied his water bucket and squatted beside the overflowing heifer. She gave him a grateful, loving glance as he began squeezing swollen teats.

It was Dil's first milk in something like six months. He dined royally on warm milk and biscuits, then rinsed out a crock his mother had left him and poured the remainder of the milk into it, entertaining fond hopes for cream, butter, maybe even cottage cheese.

Come morning he milked her again, then put a bridle to

Bill. Riding the old Chunk bareback, he began leading the heifer townward. Now where, he wondered, did Hallie Haines live? A mile down the road he suddenly knew he was not alone.

Silently he slipped off Bill's off side, gripping the 45-90 in one hand as he encouraged the horse on its way with a slap. Slipping into a clump of lodgepoles, he began paralleling the road and the meandering horse and cow. A hundred yards ahead he saw a man crouching in the brush with a rifle. The man wore a black, flat-brimmed hat and an Abraham Lincoln beard without mustache. He was watching the riderless horse and cow.

Dil oozed closer through the brush, the sound of his movement covered by Bill's noisy clip-clop and the cow's munching. He was within fifty feet of the bearded stranger now. He eased back the hammer of the 45-90, then suddenly he was struck with sudden inspiration. "Is your name Haines?" he called.

The bearded man spun and saw Dil's rifle pointed at him. Very carefully he grounded his own piece. "Yes," he said. "I'm Haines."

"I'm Dil Reeves. I found your critter last night."

"Guess I owe you an apology," Haines said. "But this goldanged country's fillin' up with some pretty queer people. Man can't be too careful."

"I've noticed that," Dil said. He lowered his rifle.

They surveyed each other for a moment. "Be nice to have some real neighbors for a change," Haines finally said. "Let's go back to the house and maybe Maw can rustle up some grub."

It sounded like the best offer Dil had heard all day.

"I hear tell Jake Nelson finally got what was comin' to him," Haines hazarded.

"So I hear," Dil conceded.

"Way I heerd it, 'twas a young feller just like you caught him tryin' to steal some horses."

"Yup."

Haines smiled a wintery smile. "My name's Al," he said. They shook hands.

"Would you have any idea who might've shot my mare?" Dil asked.

"Son of a gun! When?" Obviously Haines hadn't heard this bit of news. Dil told him.

The older man removed his flat-brimmed hat and ran a bandanna over his bald spot. "Gettin' t'where it ain't safe for decent people anymore," he muttered. "You tell the sheriff?"

Dil nodded. "Who is it winds up the spring in that little man?" he asked.

Haines thought for a moment. "Hard to tell," he said. "There's the mines up in t'other end of the county. There's the railroad. Apart from that I guess he's pretty much his own man."

"What kind of a man is that?"

Haines shrugged. "He was a good man in his day."

"Would you call him a fair man?"

"I guess so. Unless you happen to be an Indian or a Frenchman or a Negro." And that was how Dil suddenly realized that Al Haines had Quaker leanings. He guessed that the bearded man didn't lean very hard though. At least he didn't go around theeing and thouing.

They pulled into a farmyard replete with quacking ducks and geese. From somewhere came a faint odor of baking, which put Dil's nostrils aquiver. He was presented to Maw, who was a pleasant, motherly woman in a Shaker bonnet. From upstairs came mysterious commotions but no sign of the overall-clad Hallie.

It wasn't until they were sitting down to rooster and dumplings that a radiant young lady appeared, decked out in sprigged muslin. Dil stared. Finally he realized that it really was Hallie. "Mr. Reeves," she said demurely, "I owe you an apology."

"Why?"

"I was out lookin' for that cow again yesterday and three city dudes in a flivver told me they saw it up the creek at your place."

"Oh!" Dil remembered the circumstances under which he had made her father's acquaintance.

"Mr. Reeves, is something wrong?"

Dil snapped from his brown study. "I'm sorry," he said. "I was just thinkin' if another man had felt like talkin' it over he might still be alive."

"Now don't you feel bad about that," Maw comforted. "Old Jake Nelson was an evil man. He finally reaped what he sowed."

"I guess so," Dil said. He wondered what poor old Nellie had sowed to reap a small red hole between her eyes. And that reminded him that his pole wagon was still at the ford where Nellie had died.

"Why sure," Haines agreed. "I got to go in to Winville tomorrow anyhow. You ride along and we'll get your pole wagon back somehow." So what with one thing and another it was evening and Dil had no animals to tend at his own place so he figured might as well spend the night and get an earlier start for town in the morning. There wasn't any spare room in the house but there were extra sheets and blankets and there was fresh hay in the barn and before he knew it Miss Hallie was already out there making things comfortable.

She left him a lantern and said, "Just turn it down low. Paw says it's safer than strikin' a seven-day stink and havin' sparks fly everywhere."

Recalling his own misadventures with sulfur matches, Dil was inclined to agree. But he wished that Hallie would go back to the house and let him go to sleep. There was something about seeing her in sprigged muslin that was quite different from bib overalls.

"Well, I'll say good night now." Still she showed no signs of leaving.

"That was real good pie," he said.

"I'm glad you liked it. I helped Maw make it. Well, I'll say good night now."

"Yup. Good night," Dil echoed. Hallie hesitated another moment, then disappeared down the loft ladder. Perversely, once she was gone Dil wished she were back again. He sighed, wondering how a young man was supposed to act around ladies. One of these days he intended to buy a book and find out. He was nearly asleep when abruptly he sat bolt upright. "Goldang!" he exclaimed to the muttering hens, "I bet I could've kissed her!"

He didn't sleep well that night. Several times he awoke amid confused dreams of kissing Al Haines' daughter. Finally he got up and walked around the barnyard. Lady began barking immediately and her four half-grown pups joined the chorus.

Dil hightailed it back up into the loft and tried to go back to sleep. It wasn't easy with all the things he had on his mind. Finally dawn began to break. He got up again and began washing up at the horse trough.

Breakfast was grim and silent as he struggled not to yawn, now overpoweringly sleepy once the night was over. Finally he helped Al Haines harness up and they rode in to town on a buckboard, leading Bill and another Chunk behind.

"You didn't get any sight of him at all?" Haines asked.

"Huh? Oh, uh, no. I didn't see anybody."

"Hard to say who it'd be," Haines said. "Jake Nelson didn't have much truck with anybody."

They rode another quarter mile in silence before Dil

said, "Seems like those three city dudes in the flivver knew him."

"How so?"

Dil hesitated, then poured out the story about the stove. "Guess I shouldn't've done it," he concluded, "but I need a stove real bad and I figured he owed me something."

Haines was silent. "Carried one of them surveyor things on a tripod?" he asked after an interval.

"Yup."

The team and buckboard trotted smartly along a level and reasonably straight set of ruts, wheels crunching in the sandy soil. Both horses raised their tails simultaneously and the air around the buckboard became redolent. "Fartin' horse is a pullin' horse," Haines said with a grin.

They rode another mile in silence, then reached the place where Dil had always had to get off the pole wagon and take Bill and Nellie by the bridles and sweet-talk them up the hill. The thought of the old mare lying stiff, probably swollen by now, with her legs sticking up obscenely, filled him with a sudden fierce anger. "I'll get him," he muttered. "I'll find that drygulcher if it's the last thing I ever do."

Haines gave a look of Quakerly concern at Dil's language but he limited himself to saying, "I reckon you will, son. Just make sure you get the right man."

The buckboard topped the rise and they stopped to let the horses blow. Gazing at the clear, crisp forenoon, Haines said, "Gonna be a long, cold winter. How you fixed?"

"Not too good," Dil admitted. Suddenly he had that feeling again. "Got your rifle ready?" he murmured to the older man.

Haines never got a chance to answer. As Dil ducked to reach his 45-90 the bullet intended for him struck Miss Hallie's father in the right ear. The left side of Haines' head disappeared in a spray of red mist. The horses spooked and began running away with the buckboard. For a quarter mile the light rig bounced back and forth, straddling ruts. Haines' body fell half out and Dil was so busy holding on to his rifle and sawing on the reins and trying to keep low enough not to stop another bullet that he hardly noticed when the team entered another uphill stretch and this, combined with the drag of old Bill's lethargic trot behind, finally forced the exhausted and thoroughly lathered horses to settle down.

They were only a couple of miles from town now, with houses and gardens closer together. He crossed the ford and saw Nellie, swollen and her legs sticking up in the air. Beside him Haines' nearly headless body lolled where he had pulled it back up onto the seat. The bushwhacker could be miles away by now. And, once more, Dil hadn't caught so much as a glimpse.

He pulled into the end of Winville's one dusty street and saw that the sheriff's Model T roadster was parked in front of his office. As he approached the door opened and the small man came out, picking his teeth with an ivory toothpick on his watch chain.

Dil sawed the lathered horses to a halt in front of the sheriff's office. Wordlessly he pointed to what had once been Al Haines—first man to befriend him in this godforsaken country.

The sheriff's eyes were unfriendly. "I told you not to go makin' a habit of it," he said.

CHAPTER 5

Dil stared. "You miserable shypoke!" he shouted. "This is Al Haines—the only honest man in Bear Creek!"

"Then why'd you kill him?"

"I didn't!"

"Then you got no call to get all excited about it, have you?" the sheriff asked.

Dil took a deep breath and managed not to say what he felt like saying. "I reckon I do," he growled. "The way I see it, it was the same varmint as drygulched my mare. And I don't think he was after Haines. He was aimin' at me."

"You better wait inside"—the sheriff gestured at his office—"while I send somebody after Doc Goetter."

"If you was to get some men together and hurry up—" Dil began.

The sheriff gave him an impatient look. "Maybe William S. Hart does it that way," he said. "But I take a look at the map and see something over a thousand square miles without a single trail in the mountains east of here."

"But—"

"Ain't no buts about it. Besides, I ain't got no jurisdiction once you're on the reservation. Now why don't you go in there and sit down and maybe pour yourself a drink out-a the bottle you'll find in my right-hand drawer and when I get back in a few minutes you can tell me all about it."

Dil stared bleakly at the small man. Were all old men such unfeeling dastards? he wondered. Or was there something about being sheriff in a place like this that did things to a man? Maybe someday Dil would be as cold and unfeeling as this shriveled remainder of a human being. He shuddered.

Inside the sheriff's office was a potbelly stove just starting to glow. As the warmth struck his sweat-drenched clothes Dil suddenly started shivering. He sat in the sagging cane-bottomed chair opposite the sheriff's desk and tried to pull himself together. He didn't want to be shaking like this when the small man came back. But Judas Priest, didn't anybody in this town *care?*

The superheated air gave him a sudden case of the sniffles. He was angrily blowing his nose when he saw the sheriff come back with the doctor and a couple of other men. They led Al Haines' buckboard across the street to the funeral parlor and got what was left of Al inside. The sheriff came back across the street alone.

"Feelin' better now?" he asked as he came into the office.

Dil shrugged. "How'm I supposed to feel?"

The sheriff opened his desk drawer and consulted a pencil mark on the label. He looked long at Dil, then poured half a tumblerful and handed it across the desk.

Dil shook his head.

"Drink it!" the sheriff said with sudden steel in his voice.

Dil swallowed it like water. Abruptly his face changed color. He strangled and coughed several times.

"Ain't you ever drunk whiskey before?" the sheriff asked.

"Yeah," Dil lied. "But I don't want to get a taste for somethin' I can't afford." The spirit surged through his body, rising from his stomach in a warm glow until suddenly the office was entirely too hot. He unbuttoned his shirt collar and took off his hat.

"Now tell me what happened," the sheriff said. "Tell it slow from the beginning and don't leave anything out."

Dil did.

"And you didn't see nobody?"

Dil shook his head.

"Why did you duck just when the shot came?"

"I was reachin' for my rifle."

"Why?"

Dill shrugged. "I could feel it. Birds or somethin', I guess."

"Birds?"

"You know. Something strange in the woods and all at once they're quiet."

"Let's go through it again," the sheriff said.

Dil did.

The sheriff sighed and asked a few more pointless questions. Finally he shuffled some papers and said, "All right. I guess you're tellin' the truth. You can go."

"That's real white of you," Dil snarled. "What're you gonna do right now?"

"I'll investigate."

Dil gritted his teeth and tried to contain his rage. "I don't know who elects you," he said, "but I know a farm out on Bear Creek where a woman and a girl are waitin' for a man to come home. Seems t'me even if you don't want to look over where it happened the least you could do is come out there with me and tell them why Al Haines ain't never comin' home again."

The sheriff gave Dil a look of mild surprise. "I reckon you got a point," he said. "You go ahead and start out with the buckboard and I'll catch up with you in the flivver."

"I'll be expectin' you," Dil promised as he stepped outside.

The buckboard was still across the street in front of the

funeral parlor. It was colder now and there was a hint of snow in the air. It seemed doubly cold after the super-heated office. Dil backed the team from the hitching rail and headed back out of town, wondering what he was going to say to Hallie and Miz Haines. Behind, old Bill and the other spare horse clopped patiently along.

His pole wagon was still where he had left it at the ford. Nearby, Nellie's legs stuck out at odd angles as she swelled still larger. Dil tried not to look at her as he stopped the buckboard in the ford and tried to wash the blood from it. It was dried on so hard that he had to use sand.

His ear was attuned, waiting for the sound of the sheriff's tin lizzie, but there was no sound but the chattering jays. He finished scrubbing the buckboard, then guessed that as long as he was here he might as well hitch Bill and the other horse to his pole wagon. He could drive the heavy wagon and depend on the other team leading the buckboard without getting into too much trouble on the downhills. When he had harnessed up and tied a lead strap from the buckboard to the rear axle of the pole wagon there was still no sign of the sheriff.

Dil snarled and the horses' ears lay back. He went around sweet-talking them back to normal, trying not to show his rage. But one thing he was sure of. If the sheriff didn't show up before he got back to the Haines' place Dil was going back into town and find out whether his boot or the small man's pants would wear out first.

It was a long, frustrating drive back to the Haines', galloping the unladen pole wagon down hills, cursing the kind of luck that had given the buckboard team's harness only cruppers instead of breeching straps. Several times he nearly got into a tangle as the rigs threatened to catch up with one another. Several times he had to stop in hollows and sweet-talk the wall-eyed horses calm again. And the silence of the twin-rutted path through spruce and tamarack was interrupted only by the scolding of jays and whiskey jacks.

He was tempted twice by fool hens squatting under the spruce, birdbrainedly positive of their invisibility. But the churning anger within him had destroyed all appetite so he did not stop to club the succulent grouse. How was he going to break the news to Hallie and Miz Haines? It was mid-afternoon and he was within a mile of the Haines ranch when he heard the sheriff's tin lizzie coughing and rattling up the road behind him.

By then Dil had so thoroughly convinced himself that the little man was not going to show that he had to struggle to control his anger. The horses started putting on airs when they heard the flivver behind them. The sheriff saw Dil's problem and stopped. Steam jetted from the flivver's radiator. He waited until Dil was nearly into the Haines' farmyard before cranking life into the roadster and timing his entry to coincide with Dil's.

Hallie and Miz Haines stood round-eyed and silent, knowing that this visitation could bring nothing but bad news.

"Is he–?" Hallie began.

Dil nodded.

Neither woman cried. Dil wondered if it might not have been more bearable if they had.

"You must be tired," Miz Haines said. "I'll fix you somethin' to eat."

But Dil knew that they wanted to be alone with their grief. The sheriff seemed to be handling the women better than he knew how to handle Dil. Watching him, Dil was reminded of his own way of sweet-talking skittish horses.

"I better not, Miz Haines," Dil said. "I got to get my wagon home before dark. Tomorrow, if you want, I'll come back and we can all go in town together for the–" He couldn't bring himself to say the word.

Miz Haines nodded distractedly and Dil made his escape. The sheriff was still soft-soaping the women as he clucked old Bill and the borrowed horse into motion for the final uphill miles to his lean-to.

Cradling the 45-90 across his knees, he encouraged the mismatched horses along the uphill stretches. The jays and whiskey jacks scolded as shadows lengthened. Somewhere in the distance a crow cawed. He felt an instant's nerves but the crow did not repeat his warning. The team made better time than he had expected. There was still an hour of sunlight left when he reached the lean-to.

He was unhitching the horses when he abruptly realized what the crow had been talking about. That same bull elk had reappeared. Dil hesitated, regarding the magnificent rack of antlers. If he could knock it over his winter's meat was assured. Already it was freezing during the nights. He could limb off a pine and hang the meat above the fly line for a week or two.

Silently he picked up the 45-90 and started closing the range between himself and the elk. The bull's head came up from his grazing. Dil froze. After a moment the elk lowered his head again. Dil tested the wind and began circling. The elk was cautious. Each time Dil was just about in position for a shot the elk would amble on until he had a tree or a stand of brush between them.

Quite abruptly Dil realized that something was wrong. He had hunted enough to know that he was not spooking the animal. They were not alone in these woods. Dil sniffed the wind. Nothing.

He glanced about. The wind was moving very gently up the draw from the elk to him. The beast still grazed. But cautiously, raising his rack frequently to glance down the draw. Then abruptly Dil caught it: a faint, barely detectable hint of cigar smoke. He wondered momentarily what kind of an idiot would smoke while hunting, then realized that the hunter was not after the elk.

Dil fingered his rifle nervously. He had been warned. This time it was up to him to find the hunter before the hunter found him. Choosing his footing carefully, he began circling upwind, no longer stalking the bull elk.

The animal was paying no attention to him anyway; its full attention was upwind, whence the cigar smell was growing stronger. Dil backed off and made a wider circle. When he judged that he had gone far enough—and when he could no longer smell cigar smoke—he began moving back in.

The hunter had found a comfortable seat in the mossy cleft of a rock. He sat nursing a half-smoked cigar, watching the nervous elk an easy hundred yards downwind. Across his lap lay a fancy rifle whose make Dil could not recognize. After a moment he realized though that the funny long thing atop the barrel had to be a telescopic sight. The hunter was making no effort to knock over the elk.

Dil stared. He had seen this man before. This man had worn a four-cornered engineer's hat the last time Dil had seen him. He had been with two other men and some surveyor's tools in a Ford touring car. He had called Dil a rube. And now he was waiting for Dil to come blundering into his sights.

Dil was a hundred yards away, peering through a growth of autumn-shriveled fern and skunk cabbage. He had no proof. Yet he knew instinctively that this man had killed his Nellie mare—and most probably Al Haines too. He settled comfortably and began aiming the 45-90.

Abruptly the other man was alert. The elk's antlers rose and he faced them, presenting the man in the engineer's hat with a perfect shot. The stranger moved slowly from his rock saddle and positioned himself, rifle ready. The elk tossed antlers and trotted off to a safe distance. The stranger had thrown away a perfect shot.

The last doubt about whom the stranger was hunting left Dil's mind. This SOB had known Jake Nelson well enough to recognize his stove. This SOB had poisoned the hermit's mind against Dil with who knew what kind of story. Now this stranger was waiting for Dil to come in range of his sights. Dil began aiming his own rifle. He had the man's head squarely in his sights. Then he hesitated. The range was close to a hundred yards and the old 45-90 wasn't all that accurate. He lowered his sights and fixed the rifle on the gap between the stranger's shoulder blades. He began squeezing the trigger.

His eyes blurred. Suddenly he was breathing so fluttery that he couldn't hold the rifle still. He forced himself to rest. He tried again. Finally Dil had to admit to himself that he just couldn't do it. No matter what kind of a drygulcher this bastard was, Dil could not turn himself into the same kind of bastard.

The stranger must have thought he heard something. He hunched higher over the rock he was aiming from. His buttocks rose invitingly. Dil drew a bead again. He fired. Satisfaction filled his soul as he saw dust rise from the seat of the stranger's breeches. He guessed that he hadn't cut too deep, for after a single startled yelp and leap the stranger had lit running.

CHAPTER 6

Thoughtfully Dil made his way back to the lean-to. He finished unharnessing and hobbled the horses, then began putting Jake Nelson's stove back together. The job turned out to be easier than he had expected. He began trimming and fitting lodgepoles and had the fourth wall of the lean-to a foot high before the light began failing.

The flat-topped laundry stove had no oven but Dil's dutch oven nested nicely in the hole where he had removed one of the lids. He led the smokepipe out the front of the lean-to, trying to guess how he would pack mud or something around it when the wall eventually reached that height. Munching biscuits and sipping coffee, he wished that he'd had the patience to knock over a fool hen while he had the chance. Or better still, he wished that he'd had the courage of his convictions. He could just as easily have gotten the elk with one shot and the drygulching stranger with the second. He wondered if he would ever see the elk again.

Then he wondered if he would ever see the stranger again.

When he woke there was an inch of ice on the bucket. He surveyed the beginnings of the lean-to's last wall and wondered if he could finish it today, then remembered what he had to do. He got the stove going and while coffee boiled he stropped his father's razor. He wished he had better clothes but it was coming around to the time of year when a man had to wear just about anything and everything he had. Now that he had a stove at least he would be able to boil a shirt once in a while. But not, he knew, in time for today. He brushed his hat as best he could and finished his toilet. Breakfasted on coffee and last night's biscuits, he unhobbled the team and started down the road, riding old Bill and leading the Haines' horse.

Grim and dry-eyed, Miss Hallie and Miz Haines were ready and their buckboard was hitched. "No use you ridin' in on your old horse," Miz Haines said. "There's room for three."

Dil was about to accept their invitation, then he hesitated. "What's wrong?" Hallie asked.

Dil searched for a way to say it. There didn't seem to be any easy way. "I seem to draw lead," he said. "If I hadn't been sittin' beside your man we might not all be ridin' into town today."

Miz Haines nodded in sober agreement. But Hallie protested, "We ain't blamin' you."

"Maybe not," Dil said. "But I'd sure feel put out if I was to get shot at again with you ladies beside me."

There was an awkward silence. He helped them into the buckboard. "I'll stay a quarter mile or so behind," he said. Then, after a moment's thought, he added, "Miss Hallie, was it by any chance some city dude in a four-cornered hat give you the idea I might have rustled your critter?"

From her sudden flushed intake of breath Dil knew that his guess was right. "Do you know that man's name?"

"Groby," Miz Haines said. "You think he had somethin' to do with all this?"

"I don't know yet."

The buckboard pulled out of the farmyard. Dil led old Bill out, then closed the gate. The buckboard rattled on down the sandy ruts, leaving him to wonder where he had heard that name before.

It wasn't until two and a half hours later, when he was

in a crowded little chapel squinting into a hymn book and trying to decipher the third verse of "Nearer my God to Thee," that he suddenly remembered. The man who had sold him 45-90 ammunition had warned him to watch out for some son of a gun by the name of Groby.

Dil paled and nearly dropped the hymnal. My God, he thought. That was the game warden I raked across the butt! It struck him that he was getting off to a singularly bad start in Bear Creek.

His suspicion was verified when, after the chapel part was finished and they had all followed the hearse across the one-street town to the cemetery, he was finally saying his mumbled good-byes to Miz Haines and Miss Hallie.

"But you'll come home with us, won't you?" Hallie protested.

"Nobody's even lookin' for who did it," Dil reminded her. "I'll stop by later this afternoon if you don't mind." He was watching their buckboard trot briskly down Winville's one street when someone touched his sleeve. A grim-faced, middle-aged man said, "Are you Dil Reeves?"

For one frantic instant Dil was tempted to deny it. Then he shrugged. "My folks always told me I was," he admitted.

"There's a few people in town from out Bear Creek way been wantin' to say howdy. You got the time right now?"

Dil guessed he might as well get it over with. Silently he followed the stranger down the street to the hotel where he had last seen the sheriff polishing off liver and onions. The stranger led him past the empty dining room and into the bar. "I ain't a drinkin' man," Dil warned.

"So I've heard," the stranger admitted. As they stepped into the bar the half-dozen men saving shoe leather turned and studied him. "This's Dil Reeves," the stranger said.

Suddenly all was joviality as men crowded around to

shake Dil's hand and pound him on the back. What in hell is going on? he wondered.

"So you're the feller finally put a stop to old Jake," one man said and pressed an unwanted glass of whiskey into Dil's hand.

Dil was not proud of the way he had done in Jake Nelson. And the growing suspicion that both he and the hermit had been used made him less proud. Suddenly all he wanted was to get away from these adulating fools. He glanced anxiously around to see if the little sheriff was in some corner taking it all in. He wasn't, but Dil knew that there would be no way of keeping him from finding out what was happening in a town this small.

"Hear Groby, that game warden feller, come in town standin' up," somebody else hazarded.

"Straight off t'see the doctor," another cackled. "Got himself a smart one right across the ass. Way I heerd it, you coulda played checkers on his coattails gettin' out-a Bear Creek."

"You wouldn't've had nothin' t'do with that?" somebody asked slyly.

Dil looked for the door. They were still crowding him like pigs around a brood sow. In the crush he managed to spill most of the whiskey. He made a production of finishing it. "Thanks for the drink," he said and pushed for the door. "Got to tend my horse," he added and made his escape.

But once outside Dil realized that he might not have another day in town for a long time. Thoughtfully he mounted old Bill's bare back and rode to the courthouse. The land office was in a dingy room to the rear of the second floor. He edged past a well-filled garboon and stood until the eye-shaded man deigned to look up from his pencil-pushing.

"How many people filed for land up Bear Creek?" he asked.

The land office clerk shrugged. "Ten, fifteen maybe." He squinted. "You filed for a section up there two, three months ago, didn't you? Let's see. Don't tell me. Uh—Reeves!" he triumphed.

"That's right," Dil said. "Is there any more land left to file on?"

"Well, I guess you could say yes. Proper question would be, is there any more up there worth filin' on?"

"Is there?" Dil asked.

The clerk pushed back his eye shade and shrugged again. "There again, it'd be a matter of opinion. You been up there long enough to see what it's like. You want to withdraw your application?"

Dil stared at the clerk.

The clerk gave a conspiratorial smile. "Handle it right and I could just sort of lose the papers. That way you'd still be able to homestead somewhere else if you ever find a good piece of land."

Dil wondered if this was legal. He suspected that it was not. "Has anybody else filed on any land since I have?" he asked.

"Lots of young fellers make a mistake, decide it ain't what they want after all. Seems a shame a feller's only got one chance to homestead," the clerk said.

"How about it?" Dil asked.

"How about what? You want me to lose the papers?"

"How about letting me see the maps," Dil said. "I want to see if anybody's filed on any vacant sections since I did."

"Oh." The clerk was crestfallen. For a moment Dil thought that the eye-shaded man was going to refuse him a look at the maps.

"I'd take it as real unneighborly if'n anybody was to

lose any copy of the papers that ought to've been filed in Washington already," he said with an edge to his voice.

The clerk gave up and let him see the maps. Two sections upcreek from Dil's had names penned in. Dil squinted and read "Jas. Sprague" on the section next to his. The one after that belonged to W. Breedon. Dil closed his eyes and tried to visualize the land upcreek from him. "Why, a man couldn't spread out a bedroll there without stilts to one side," he muttered. "Why would anybody want to homestead a mountainside?"

"I told you that country's no good," the clerk said. "You want me to lose the papers?"

"You do," Dil said, "and I just might get to thinkin' you're tied in somehow with the drygulchers that are tryin' to force me out of there."

"Oh no!" The clerk was horrified. "You want to stay, that's your right."

"This Sprague and Breedon," Dil continued, "what kind of men are they?"

"I don't remember," the clerk hastened.

Dil looked steadily at him. The clerk's face was suddenly ashen.

"You know," Dil said, "in this state they hang people for murder."

The man in the eye shade looked like he was going to faint.

"Now I'll ask you again," Dil pressed. "What do Sprague and Breedon look like?"

The clerk swallowed and his Adam's apple jerked up and down several times.

Dil was struck with a sudden inspiration. "Would they by any chance be a couple of city dudes with funny hats and surveying stuff—couple of jim dandies that go chasin' 'round the country in a flivver with our own Mr. Groby?"

From the sudden trapped look in the clerk's eyes Dil

knew that he had hit pay dirt. He considered squeezing more information out of the frightened man but suddenly the clerk was gasping and clutching his chest. Dil didn't believe it, but then he didn't much care. He spun and stalked out of the land office.

Moments later, from his vantage point around the corner of the building, he saw the man, still wearing his green eye shade, come tearing out of the courthouse and make a beeline for the sheriff's office.

Dil smiled a wintery smile and checked his 45-90. He mounted old Bill and rode the hundred yards to the sheriff's office. The blinds were drawn against the afternoon sun so he took his time tying Bill to the hitching rail. He considered carrying the rifle inside, then decided that it might be considered plumb unneighborly. He leaned it against the hitching rack, then stalked to the door. He threw it open without knocking.

The small man with the star gave him an unruffled glance. The clerk gave him the same look of horror and guilt Dil had once seen in a dog caught sucking eggs.

Dil stood in the doorway, staring down at the two men. The potbellied stove was glowing. The air was superheated. He felt sweat start to trickle.

"I gotta go," the clerk blurted. "I'll see you later."

"Yup, you do that," the sheriff said in serene tones. Turning to Dil, he added, "Sit down. Take a load off your feet. I hear you been busy."

"Reckon I have," Dil said. "How about you? You got any idea who shot my horse, who shot Al Haines, and who stirred up old Jake Nelson against me?"

"Nope," the sheriff said. "You got any idea who burnt a crease on some city hunter? Just might be the same person."

Dil sensed that the little man was laughing at him. He

wondered what would happen if he kicked the smug son of a gun up and down the one street of Winville.

"Sit down," the sheriff repeated. "I been wantin' to talk with you."

"Yeah?" Dil countered. "About what?" It was getting hotter and hotter in this tight room. He unbuttoned his shirt.

"Make yourself comfortable," the sheriff said. "This may take a while. I want you to think it over good before you answer."

"I been doin' a lot of thinkin'," Dil growled.

"No doubt you have," the sheriff said. "Leastways as much thinkin' as anybody twenty-three years old can be expected to think."

"How'd you know how old I am?"

"I know a lot about you," the sheriff said. "And I know you ain't fixed too well to spend the winter out on Bear Creek. How'd you like a job and a chance to earn some cash money in town?"

Dil wondered when the trap was going to spring. "I'd have to stay out there enough to make good my homestead claim," he said.

The sheriff shrugged. "I s'pose it could be arranged but I'm damned if I can see if all Bear Creek's worth it."

"What kind of a job?" Dil asked.

"Deputy. I'm sixty-one years old," the sheriff said. "Gettin' tired of this kind of job. You do a good job and you just might be sheriff come next election."

CHAPTER 7

Dil stared, wondering where the hook was. It had to be somewhere. He wondered if he was getting too close and they were buying him off. Somehow it didn't sound right. Men who had not hesitated to do in old Jake Nelson or Al Haines wouldn't be getting chicken-hearted now.

"I don't know," he managed. "I ain't never thunk about bein' a lawman."

"Pays good," the sheriff said. There was a long silence. The office was sweltering. Dil wondered if the old man was sick. Something had to be wrong with him to want to live in this kind of heat. The silence grew between them. But the sheriff seemed unruffled, not really caring all that much which way Dil answered.

Finally Dil could stand the heat no more. "Got to be gettin' on," he muttered.

The sheriff nodded. "Take your time," he said. "But come back and let me know within a week."

"I will," Dil said. As he was opening the door the sheriff added, "If you're goin' out to Bear Creek tonight, maybe you could find some different road. I'd hate t'see you git kilt before you made up your mind."

Dil nodded soberly. Outside the office it was growing dark. He thought of the long, slow, uphill ride under the shadow of spruce and jackpines. Thoughtfully he picked up his rifle. He was mounting Bill when he abruptly realized why it felt wrong. He opened the chamber and discovered that the 45-90 was empty.

He controlled himself and rode out of town wondering if anyone had seen him inspect the ancient Winchester. When the houses of Winville were disappearing in the dusk he rummaged through his pockets. Son of a beagle! Crawling through the brush after that bushwhacker yesterday he must have lost several rounds. He patted his pockets again, inventorying pants, shirt, coat. He had two rounds to see him home. And the sheriff had warned him to look out.

For an instant he considered the sheriff's offer. Maybe he ought to go back and demand a star, a pair of pistols, and a cash advance on his salary. But somebody had done in Al Haines. Dil wasn't yet sure who but he didn't want his hands tied if it turned out to be who he thought it was. To hell with the little sheriff's cheap try at buying him!

There were, he realized, distinct disadvantages to being poor. The bit of whiskey he had not been able to avoid drinking had served excellently to remind him that he had not eaten since morning. With a spare dollar or two he could eat and spend the night at the hotel. As it was he didn't even have blankets with him. He gritted his teeth and continued riding toward Bear Creek.

It was well dark by the time he reached the ford. Nellie's legs stuck grotesquely in the air, outlined in the quarter moon. He hurried past and into the impenetrable blackness of the timber, wishing he could make some practical use of the sheriff's advice. But the next thirteen miles, apart from a half-mile stretch past the pothole, would be enclosed in a velvety blackness as impenetrable as a cow's insides. If somebody was laying for him it ought to make things just as hard for them as for Dil himself.

He gave old Bill his head, hoping that the Chunk would know the way home better than he. They clopped along in companionable silence for another couple of miles. At places where the rutted path straightened for a hundred yards he managed an occasional glimpse of the frost-ringed moon. It was getting colder and he was grateful for old Bill's warm bare back. Somewhere in the darkness the sudden shriek of a screech owl raised his hackles and he sensed Bill's nerves getting on edge too.

He thought about getting off the road again but knew that he wouldn't make ten paces before a low branch put out an eye or scraped him off. Even here on the road the horse seemed to be having trouble, occasionally stumbling as his wide hooves missed the rut. Soon there would be snow, and another expense—he would have to ride back in to Winville and have old Bill sharpshod. Dil tried to look on the bright side. With Nellie gone he only needed half as much hay. Maybe he could spend these last few days before snowfall cutting poles and clearing. After snow maybe he could sleigh a few poles into town with Bill alone. Or maybe work out a deal with Al Haines to borrow his horse. Then he remembered that he was coming home from Al Haines' funeral.

He had told the Haines women that he would stop in on the way home but it would be way past bedtime, he knew, before he reached their turn-off. Somewhere deep in the woods a fox yapped. Bill snorted and blew, then clopped off another patient mile before a rabbit made its last shrill complaint against the world's injustice. Dil heard the crunch of bones. Which reminded him that if that bunch of city dudes was going to keep prowling around spoiling his hunting he was going to have to see about setting some snares for cottontails and snowshoes. With any luck the skins might make coffee-and-salt money through the winter. Come spring, by God, he was going to get in a crop!

Slowly the night hours devoured the miles up the winding Bear Creek road. He was just approaching the pothole in the clearing where he had scared up the loon the other day when Bill snorted again. A moment later Dil sniffed it too, a faint hint of something totally alien to the dark and silent woods. He wrinkled his nose, puzzled for a moment, then recognized the benzine-buggy stink of an automobile. Abruptly he remembered the sheriff's warning.

It was too late now. They had heard old Bill's dinner-plate-sized hooves clopping along the sandy road. They had heard the old horse blow. In the three months Dil had lived up Bear Creek he had seen only two automobiles on this road. One was the sheriff's roadster yesterday, coming out to break the news to Miz Haines and Miss Hallie. The other had carried three strangers in four-cornered hats and a transit.

Dil peered into the darkness and saw nothing. He was at the edge of the clearing. The quarter moon had moved until half of the clearing was in shadow but Dil could guess how the strangers would have set it up. They were waiting in the shadows at the opposite side of the clearing, waiting for him to ride out into the moonlight. Dil felt his hackles rise.

"Whoa, Bill," he called. "Just take it easy, old hoss, and I'll get that rock out-a your frog." Sweet-talking the horse, he moved back from the clearing and into the woods, making as much noise as a small army as Bill blundered through a patch of brittle sumac. Still sweet-talking his horse, he was tying him to a tree when abruptly he changed his mind. If things went wrong he didn't want his blameless horse to die of thirst and hunger. He unsnapped the bit from one side and left old Bill noisily cropping grass, the bit jingling with each move.

Meanwhile Dil worked his cautious way back to the edge of the clearing, where trees shadowed the setting moon. Moving as quietly as he could through the grass, he oozed toward the place where he thought the road continued on up Bear Creek through the trees. The smell of gasoline grew stronger. Sweat trickled down Dil's shoulder blades as he crept through the autumn-dry grass at the edge of the clearing. Each time he moved grass rustled until he was sure that it could be heard clear to the Haines'.

He gave silent thanks that it was too cold for snakes to be out. Somewhere in the shadows he heard the faint creak of leather and seat springs. He wondered if he dared try to get nearer. Somebody was whispering nervously and he realized that the silence had lasted too long for him to be prying a pebble from old Bill's hoof. He scrabbled blindly in the grass and found a pine cone. It took him a small eternity to find another. Finally he was ready, prone in the grass with rifle pointed. He squinted at the shadowy skyline, trying to find the notch where the downhill road continued through the trees. He tossed a pine cone. Immediately he tossed the other.

Suddenly the clearing was flooded with light as the car's headlights came on. Dil was half dazzled but not as helpless as he would have been if he had blundered into the lower end of the clearing, where the lights pointed. He couldn't see clearly behind the headlights but, aiming by instinct, he squeezed off one shot.

The venerable 45-90 roared like a small cannon, echoes reverberating from hill to hill. Immediately the lights went off. "You son of a bitch!" somebody shrieked. "You told me his gun was empty!"

In the darkness Dil heard the sounds of vigorous cranking. The motor roared to life. There were grinding sounds and a moment later the lightless auto was tearing across the clearing, heading back down the road toward Winville. Dil lay shuddering in the grass, acutely aware of his remaining ammunition. He wondered what he would have done if they had fanned out to hunt him down properly.

When he was through shaking he walked back across the clearing and whistled until old Bill snorted and gave some hint of where he was hidden in the shadows. Moments later Dil was riding the remaining miles uphill to his lean-to.

The dew had abruptly changed to hoarfrost and Bill's hooves crunched each time he missed the sandy rut and stepped on grass. It was dead calm and silent. The moon went down completely. The horse was stumbling more frequently now. Dil's nerves slowly unwound, leaving him with a bone tiredness that made it hard to stay atop the Chunk's broad bare back. From time to time he caught the gurgle of Bear Creek. The forest's inhabitants seemed to have settled down for the night. Dil guessed that it would be at least three more miles before he could.

Finally he was approaching the lean-to. Bill had increased his pace as he got closer to home but as they approached the lean-to the old horse stopped and snorted again. Dil wrinkled his nose once more as he caught the whiff of gasoline. Now what, he wondered, had those varmints planned for him here? For one panic-stricken moment he was afraid that they'd burned his cabin, then he saw its reassuring bulk loom dark and silent under the pines.

Somewhere he had a lantern with a little coal oil left in it. But the gasoline smell was so strong that he was afraid to light a match. The thought of blundering into God knew what kind of a trap was even more terrifying. But he had to get his blankets or he would freeze to death before morning. Already he was shivering now that he was separated from the old horse's broad, warm back.

Finally he had Bill hobbled and unbridled. He found a six-foot piece of frondy lodgepole top and, waving and sweeping it before him, crept into his inky-black lean-to. Inside, the gasoline stink was not so strong. They hadn't tried to burn him out, he guessed. The stink was just from the way those gas buggies always dribbled and dripped whenever they stopped for a while. But Dil also knew perfectly well that they had not been here on any friendly errand. He shook out his blankets on the odd chance of a frost-chilled rattler having been planted where his body heat could revive it. There was nothing.

He gave a gusty sigh and pulled off his boots. Trying not to move anything else, he crawled between his blankets. Somewhere off behind the cabin he could hear old Bill sigh.

Morning was bright and clear with the frost almost melted off before hunger woke him. He pulled his stiff boots back on and walked awkwardly down to the creek for a bucket of water. There was still firewood from his cabin carpentry. He opened the laundry stove to poke down the ashes before starting a breakfast fire and discovered that he had already done so.

Then abruptly he realized that he had not yet heard old Bill this morning. Panic shot through him at the realization that they must have planted something to do in his last horse. He walked in broadening circles around the lean-to, whistling and calling the horse while slowly his boots thawed and made walking less of a torture.

He was a quarter mile up the creek from the cabin when he saw fresh-dug dirt. Someone had been digging into a side hill. He approached cautiously but there was nothing there—just an open hole a couple of feet into the cut bank.

He studied the hole for several minutes without learning anything more. It was a hole. Nothing buried in it, no effort at concealment. Still puzzled, he continued up the creekbank, calling and whistling.

The country grew increasingly vertical and the creek's noise louder as it rushed over rock ledges and crashed into pools. Finally there was an actual waterfall some fifteen feet high. Dil realized that he was out of his own section now, upstream in the new homesteads claimed by Sprague and Breedon. He found another hole, this time only a foot deep, where shovels had scarred bedrock. Then he realized that the scars were from chipping hammers taking samples. He wondered if Winville had an assay office. Maybe he should have looked into this possibility instead of telegraphing things to the clerk in the land office.

By now the country was impossible for old Bill and nearly impossible for Dil. He walked slowly down the creek toward his lean-to, wondering what had happened to his horse. When he reached the lean-to Bill was placidly munching frost-seared grass a few yards away.

Dil felt like kicking himself. Half of the morning wasted chasing around looking at somebody else's fool holes in the ground when he ought to have known that old Bill was smart enough to come home when he felt like it. He went back to the stove and began laying a fire. His stomach was growling with the realization that it had been something over twenty-four hours since he had last eaten.

He was searching his pockets for a match when it hit him. They had been up here prowling around his lean-to. He remembered the gasoline stink from where they must have parked their flivver for some time. Yet nothing had been disturbed. Except . . .

I didn't shake down those ashes, he remembered. *That stove was still hot when I went off to Al Haines' funeral!* Holding his breath, he began carefully pulling his kindling piece by piece out of the stove. Then he realized that the half-burnt-out grate had been clean. He opened the ash door on the bottom.

The ashes in the tray were far too high for a single meal cooked in this stove. And too carefully leveled. He took a deep breath and began slowly pulling out the ash drawer. A piece of heavy string emerged from the ashes, snaking around nearly out of sight and up into the back of the grate.

Dil followed the cord down into the ashes. It was primacord. Buried in the ash drawer were four sticks of forty percent Hercules blasting powder, each with its own Excelsior cap.

CHAPTER 8

Still holding his breath, Dil got out his jackknife and dug the caps from the sticks of dynamite. Somebody had done a professional job, puncturing the wrapper with a cedar pencil point, crimping the caps over the primacord with a careful closing of molars. He carried the explosives off a hundred yards and stowed them in the hollow under the roots of a hillside pine. Then, wondering whether it had been planned as a final solution or merely as a warning, he went back and looked at the stove, studying where the top end of the fuse had been.

With luck and slow-burning kindling he could have been doing his chores a hundred yards away before the fire reached the fuse. Or could it? He pawed through the ashes and recognized the sprinkling of what looked like black pepper. It was around the fire box of the square-topped stove too. He whittled a spill of pitchy shavings on the end of a pole and lit them. When he stuck the torch in the open stove there was a whoosh. Flames shot skyward and the stovepipe fell down. But the stove was now burned clean of black powder. He guessed that he could go ahead with breakfast.

He spent the interval while biscuits were baking poking carefully through the lean-to, looking for other surprises, but he found none. They had either not found or not bothered with his store of 45-90 cartridges. What with the attrition of the last few days he had only twelve left.

As the coffee boiled he picked the rocks out of beans.

Cooking them was an all-day job at this altitude but he figured that if he boiled them for an hour in the morning and another in the evening, three days from now they might approach edibility. And he was getting goldarned sick of biscuits.

By evening he had the fourth wall of the lean-to within a foot of the roof and was growing increasingly desperate for a solution to the problem of how to close the gap around the stovepipe without setting fire to the lodgepoles. All that evening he sat huddled next to the stove, nursing the beans along and thinking about how to close the wall, about who had tried to kill him, and about the sheriff. He couldn't figure out the little man. He didn't seem to like Dil, yet he had offered him a job. The small aging man didn't seem to feel anything at all. Dil wondered if perhaps he had seen too many things to ever dare to involve himself.

He was drifting off to sleep when abruptly the solution to his stovepipe problem struck him. Next morning he went back to the hillside pine and removed one stick of powder and a cap. Down by the creekbank he planted the charge under a ledge of some kind of stratified sedimentary rock and lit a short piece of primacord. Seconds later he had the raw material to build a stone transition through his lodgepole wall.

He was carrying the rectangular, brick-shaped pieces of rock back to the lean-to when he heard a flivver struggling up the sandy-soiled ruts. Now what, he wondered, was the sheriff doing out here so soon? Then abruptly he realized that it was most probably not the sheriff. Whoever had planted that blasting powder in his stove had heard the explosion and was coming back to make sure. Dil hastily dropped his armload of rocks and scooted back to the lean-to. He caught up his rifle and kept on moving until he was hidden in the hillside timber above his humble home.

The car labored uphill, emitting that peculiar howling moan of a flivver with a worn low-gear band. Dil jacked a round into the 45-90.

But when the flivver arrived it was a top-down touring car he had never seen before. Three men in pepper-and-salt suits stopped at the entrance to his place. After milling indecisively for a moment about the steaming radiator they began walking up the path toward his lean-to.

The men walked funny. Dil studied their tight-fitting suits and concluded that if they were armed their pistols were very small. He could not figure out what their odd walk reminded him of until the three men were nearly at his lean-to. Then as one glanced up the hill toward his hiding place the sun caught his broad, dark face. The men were Indians. "Anybody home?" one yelled.

They waited in the open, making no effort to poke or pry. "Anybody home?" the taller one called again. They waited another minute, then shrugged and began walking back to the car. Dil guessed that was proof enough of honest intentions. He came down the hill making plenty of noise. The three dark men saw him and waited. As he came near one consulted a scrap of paper. "Are you Mr. Reeves?" he asked.

Dil was mildly astonished to hear perfect, and what he had always thought of as Boston, English emanating from this man instead of the usual mouth-full-of-potatoes struggle when the red man tackled English. "Yes," he said, "I'm Dil Reeves."

"I'm Joe Spokane," the tall Indian said. "This is Henry Hawkins and this is Edward Weeks. We represent the tribal council."

"What can I do for you?" Dil asked.

"It's rather complicated," the tall Indian said. "But something has come up that can harm us both. We're trying to enlist some cooperation between the Bear Creek people and the inhabitants of the reservation."

It took Dil a moment to realize that he meant Indians. He waited for the tall man to continue.

"Do you realize that Bear Creek originates some thirty miles east of here, well inside the reservation?"

"I never thought about it," Dil said. "I guess it's reasonable." He glanced upstream, remembering the increasing verticality of the country in that direction.

The Indian–what was his name? Joe Spokane, Dil remembered–said, "I've some ordnance maps in the car. If you've a few minutes to spare perhaps it would clarify things to look at the relative elevations."

Dil followed the trio back to the steaming flivver, hoping that he would understand what Spokane was saying once he got a look at the maps. Where, he wondered, did an Indian ever learn to use all these six-bit words?

The trio extracted a rolled map from the back seat of the flivver and spread it over the front fender. Dil wondered what all the wavy lines were. They seemed to spread out at the top and bottom of the map. Toward the center they converged and actually ran into one another. "Are you familiar with ordnance maps?" Joe Spokane asked.

"Been a while since I seen one," Dil admitted.

"These lines represent equal elevations." The Indian looked at Dil. "Heights," he amended. "It's like drawing a line as level as you can around the hillside."

"Looks like you got a canyon in the middle there," Dil said.

"Exactly. Now here"–he pointed at a spot some distance below the gorge–"is your section, where we're standing now."

Dil studied the map, remembering his morning stroll upstream looking for Bill. He guessed that he must have been approaching the bottom of the region where the hour glass pinched together. The tall Indian seemed to be waiting for him to digest this information. Dil looked up.

"Bear Creek drops one hundred eighty feet in three miles." He continued with some bushwah about flow rates that was completely over Dil's head.

Dil waited for the Indian to get to the point.

"Can you imagine what would happen to Bear Creek Valley if someone were to erect a dam at this point?" He indicated the place where all the contour lines converged a few miles upstream from Dil's section.

Dil thought for a moment. "I dunno," he admitted. "Guess I wouldn't much like livin' under a dam and wonderin' every time it rained if the thing was gonna let go on top of me." He thought for another minute. "They gonna cut off all our water?"

Joe Spokane ignored his question for the moment. "The impounded waters—lake," he amended, "will cover approximately this area." He indicated a red-inked portion that covered a good part of the top of the map. "Only one third of the reservation's area," the Indian continued, "but the only arable portions thereof. If this dam goes in we shall be reduced to living on hillsides and mountaintops." He hesitated for another moment, then added, "And you people of Bear Creek Valley—"

"What about us?" Dil asked.

"Several things could happen to you, depending on how well built the dam is, and, more importantly, for whom and what it's built."

Dil glanced at Bear Creek's scant dozen feet of width. In the spring, when snow was melting off, the flow was larger, but still . . . "I can't see anybody botherin' with a little stream like that to make electricity," he said. "Some of those flatland wheat farmers gonna put in apples or somethin'?"

"At first that was what we thought," Spokane said. He paused and wiped his face with a white handkerchief. "Mr. Reeves," he continued, "have you ever had any dealings with the federal government?"

"Some," Dil said. "I filed on this section and once I mailed a letter."

Joe Spokane almost smiled. "Unfortunately we have been forced to learn the labyrinthine ways of Washington. If it serves no other purpose, the Bureau of Indian Affairs has, at the very least, educated some few of us in the ways of bureaucracy."

Dil gave a mental sigh and waited for the tall Indian to simmer down and make sense again.

"I and my colleagues squandered tribal funds for nearly two months in Washington, chasing from office to bureau to office. If I may be permitted a liberty, some of you people—especially those in your nation's capital—have a propensity for speaking with a forked tongue."

It took Dil a moment to work all this out. Then he remembered the clerk in the Winville land office. He guessed that the Indian just might have a point. "What'd you find out?" he asked.

"No one in this vale of tears," Joe Spokane seemed to be getting up a head of steam, "can ever be absolutely sure when even the eternal verities alter from day to day. But in this case, the government's sincere and heartfelt professions of profound ignorance with reference to any dam foolishness in this area seem reasonably well founded."

Dil sorted this out for a moment. "You mean the government ain't buildin' the dam?"

"Apparently not."

"So who is?"

Joe Spokane shrugged. "Riparian law and anything pertaining to water rights achieves a Byzantine complexity unmatched even by the fine print of an Indian treaty.

Since tribal funds are not unlimited we were forced to return home."

"You don't know?" Dil thought for a moment. "But hell," he protested, "the reservation belongs to you. Wouldn't that Indian bureau or whatever it is know if anybody was damming up a reservation?"

"Were it not for the principle of benign neglect overlaid on bureaucratic incompetence and laziness, this might be the case," Spokane said. "But unfortunately the dam itself is being planned just outside the boundaries of reservation land. Only the lake will invade us. And we may well be drowned before the obscure records of some out-of-the-way courthouse yield the incriminating but no doubt perfectly legal documents."

Dil was having heavy going with the Indian's prolix rendition of Clarence Darrow. "I'd like to help you," he said, "but I been havin' troubles of my own."

"Oh?" Joe Spokane was sudden silence and sympathy. Dil glanced at the other two, shorter Indians dressed in identical salt-and-pepper suits. He wondered if it was some kind of a uniform. "Do you understand English?" he asked the silent pair. They nodded and smiled.

"You've been having troubles, Mr. Reeves?" the tall Indian pursued. "Is there anything we can do to help?"

Dil didn't know. But this trio was so different from the firewater-ruined souses he had always associated with their race that suddenly he was pouring out all his problems into their sympathetic ears.

"And the sheriff has done nothing to help you?" Spokane asked.

"Well . . ." Dil didn't know what he felt about the sheriff. The scholarly-appearing little man with pince-nez and sheepskin vest had, he remembered, warned him about a possible ambush the night coming home from Al Haines' funeral. Maybe this, he guessed, was what Joe Spokane meant by "benign neglect."

"And your other Bear Creek neighbors?" the Indian pursued. "Has anyone tried to force them out?"

"I don't know," Dil said. "Unless you figure somehow somebody didn't really care whether Jake Nelson got me or I got him." He paused. "Apart from the Haineses, I don't know anybody else in Bear Creek. Been tryin' to get set for winter."

"Why don't you take the sheriff's offer of a job?"

Dil shrugged. "I dunno. Guess I just never thought about bein' a lawman. Somehow it just don't seem right."

"Perhaps not," the Indian said. "But at present you have no—" He hesitated. "Ah yes, I see. You suspect the sheriff may know more than he says about this affair and you mistrust him."

"Don't you?"

The Indian shrugged. "After two months in Washington all white men start looking alike," he said. "But consider: In your present position your impotence approaches totality. If you were to accept the sheriff's offer at least you would be in a position to learn certain things. And if you disliked what you saw you could always quit."

"My *what* approaches *what?*" Dil asked.

"Your hands are tied," Spokane explained. "Out here you can't do anything to defend yourself. In town . . ." He left it dangling. Dil still stared at him. "In any event," Spokane continued, "our problems may be interconnected. We shall be flooded. You shall be washed out. We have a common enemy."

"Not unless the dam breaks we won't be washed out," Dil protested. "Maybe they'll build it good."

"Maybe," the Indian said. "But put all your bits of information together and what do you see? The dam is not big enough for hydroelectric power. There is no place near worth irrigating. And somebody has been digging test holes in lower Bear Creek."

Dil paled and for a moment he thought that he was going to have to sit down. "Jesus!" he finally wheezed. "The hydraulickers!"

CHAPTER 9

Ogres of the western states, the hydraulickers had forever ruined whole counties in California and Alaska. Now they were going to wash Dil's homestead downstream, leaving behind a bare rock mass, piling sand, soil, and gravel in spoil banks miles downstream, forever retired from any hope of agriculture.

Dil thought for a moment. So there was gold here—or whatever precious metal they wanted to mine. If there was it had to be in such minute amounts that he could never recover it himself without using hydraulic equipment. Only somebody with the capital for dam building could get the gold out—out of Dil's land, out of the Haines'—out of Jake Nelson's proven-up homestead too. He wondered if it was general cussedness that had induced the hermit to try to kill him—or if the giant had been led to believe that he was in league with the hydraulickers.

"Do you now see that we have something in common?" Joe Spokane asked.

Dil nodded dumbly. "But what can I do?" he asked. "Nobody can stop hydraulickers."

"They are only men," Spokane said.

Dil's whole folklore and breeding told him that this was not so. Hydraulickers were a special breed: irresistible, vicious, satanic in their single-minded destruction of the environment. Compared to them, sheepmen were harbingers of light. Hydraulickers, it was darkly whispered among aunts and mothers, were responsible both for Papa's disappearance in the Klondike and for the disappearance of any documents pertaining to his claim. But the Indian was still talking.

"Being men, they are also subject to the slings and arrows of an outraged citizenry."

"You goin' on the warpath?" Dil asked.

"Only by strictly legal means," Spokane said. "In any contest at arms we have an unfortunate history of coming out second best." He wiped his forehead again. "It is not without some difficulty that I have persuaded some of my older compatriots that our only hope is through adaptation to the Byzantine intrigues of the Great White Father."

It was the first time that Dil had ever heard "Great White Father" pronounced with just that satirical intonation. Suddenly his mind caught up with the evidence in front of him. Indians, he suddenly realized, were not all irresponsible drunkards. They must be just people like everybody else he knew. Some smarter than others. And if the government was immovable when it came to protecting the rights of poor white men, what must it be like to be an Indian? Astonished, Dil saw a whole new world of insight opening before him. "You really think you can stop 'em?" he asked.

"If the inhabitants of lower Bear Creek will unite with us there may be a chance. Will you help?"

"I'll do what I can," Dil said.

"Will you accept the sheriff's offer and keep your eyes and ears open?"

"Guess I'll have to if I'm gonna eat this winter," Dil said reluctantly.

The three Indians smiled. "The position will give you a chance to get around and meet your neighbors," Spokane continued. "There is where you can be a real help."

"How?"

"You have an honest face," Spokane said. "For 'honest' read 'white.' "

"What do you want me to do?"

"Use that honest face to convince your neighbors that we must all work together if we are to survive."

"Ain't gonna be easy," Dil admitted. "Lots of folks don't like Indians."

"Nothing worthwhile is ever easy," Spokane said. "Lots of Indians feel no overweening fondness for the spoilers of their ancestral hunting grounds. But the past is the past. If either of us are to survive we must look to the future."

To Dil it sounded suspiciously like Fourth of July oration but he could find no holes in the Indian's argument. "All right," he said, "I'll do it." He stuck out his hand. As the three Indians in pepper-and-salt suits shook it he tried to read their expressions. They seemed friendly and sympathetic but he couldn't help feeling that they were somehow amused. It seemed almost as if they were the white men patronizing some poor stupid Indian.

He watched bemusedly as one of the silent Indians cranked life into the flivver and they began bouncing and lurching back toward Winville. Still somewhat dazed by what had happened, he glanced at the sky. It was still before noon. If he pushed old Bill he could be in town before dark. And if the sheriff was serious he would have to see about finding lodgings in town anyhow. He gazed regretfully at the still unfinished lean-to, but . . . this was the only solution. If he tried to go it alone out here the bushwhackers would get him sooner or later. His only hope was to identify them positively. It wouldn't hurt him, he guessed, to have a badge. And a pistol, and some ammunition, and some new boots, and a square meal.

He was a mile down the road when he remembered that he had not stopped in on the Haines women after the funeral. He gave the sun a glance and guessed that there was time. It was turning colder and the bright sun of early morning had disappeared. Dil looked worriedly at the clouds, hoping that it wouldn't snow. Bill was snorting and prancing from the brisk weather, holding his tail high, as if he had been gingered for trading.

In spite of all the things that had happened to him Dil was in an optimistic mood. Somehow, he knew, he would survive. Hadn't he somehow survived since Papa had failed to come home from the Klondike? He remembered the lean years of hardscrabble peddling berries and vegetables from the five acres Mama had struggled so desperately to hang on to—until finally the burgeoning metropolis of Spokane had half surrounded the farm, until by some unexplained maneuver in city hall the taxes had abruptly increased tenfold and Mama had quietly died.

Dil remembered most vividly the day the deputies had moved Mama's furniture out into the street and his own frantic rush to escape the hell hole they called an orphanage. And now he was on his way to become a deputy. He would quit, he firmly resolved, before he would be a part of moving any widow out into the street. He was still gritting his teeth when he turned down the lane into the Haines' farmyard.

Miz Haines and Miss Hallie, who managed to look quite attractive even in bib overalls, were both in the yard doing chores when he arrived. They looked worn and drawn, Miz Haines especially. Miss Hallie's face lit up momentarily as she saw Dil approach, then she went back to shooing chickens into an enclosure.

"I'd've come yesterday," Dil began, "but I didn't get home from town till late." Then abruptly he noticed the torn fences. "What happened?" he asked.

Miz Haines sighed. "When we got home yesterday—" She broke off and waved.

"They make off with much?" Dil asked.

"They run off the horses and the cow and half the chickens," Hallie said. She sounded as if she was struggling not to cry. "And–" Wordlessly she pointed at the barn.

Dil went in. The bitch and her half-grown pups were dead, mother shot and the younger dogs clubbed and pitchforked to death. Dil found a shovel. Wordlessly he found a bare spot in the wilted flowerbed outside Miz Haines' kitchen window and began burying the dogs.

He was nearly finished before Hallie appeared, red-eyed but in control. "You got any idea who?" Dil asked.

She shrugged.

Miz Haines appeared. "Come inside and have some coffee," she said. "I'm sorry we ain't got no more milk to put in it."

They sat glum and silent around the kitchen table. Finally Miz Haines looked at Dil. "Don't feel bad about yesterday," she said. "You're still a young man and young men have to feel their oats once in a while."

Dil stared, wondering what she was talking about. The silence grew. Finally Miz Haines broke it again. "All those men in the saloon, I mean. They're mostly good people. They're hardpressed as the rest of us. Ain't nobody goin' to begrudge you a drink or two in a warm place."

"But I didn't–" Dil began. Then he realized that they had no way of knowing what had happened to him. "I wonder if the people who cleaned you out are the same ones went through my place," he mused.

While the women listened in growing alarm he told them about the ambush on the way home and the blasting powder in his stove. Such being the power of possession, he hardly noticed that already it was *his* stove. "By the way," he finished, "did you happen to see three Indians come by in a tin lizzie this morning?"

"Yes," Miz Haines said through thin lips. "Offered to help find my stock and I give 'em what for. Varmint savages do it whenever they run out of drinking money—run off your stock and then go find it for a dollar!"

Dil guessed that now was not the time to broach the subject. Instead he said, "The sheriff offered me a cash-money job."

"What?" They were instantly suspicious.

"Deputy."

Both women gasped and unconsciously drew back.

"You gonna take it?" Hallie finally asked.

Dil shrugged. "Didn't want to," he said. He searched for a way to explain and finally decided that he had no talent for the devious. "I had quite a long talk with those Indians." He hesitated. "They sounded pretty honest to me."

Miz Haines wasn't throwing things at him so Dil went on to explain what the Indians had told him. When he had finished both women were silent. "They actually asked you to take the job?" Miz Haines finally asked.

"Way I see it, somebody's gonna get the job. You know somebody else you'd ruther see's deputy?"

Apparently neither Miz Haines nor Miss Hallie did. Yet both still had qualms, regarding any such government job, with the possible exception of mailman, as trading with the enemy. Before he had time to get used to the idea, he was spending the night.

"You goin' on in to town today?" Miss Hallie finally asked next morning.

She was red-eyed and still wearing bib overalls and a blue chambray shirt which, from its size, Dil suspected had belonged to Al Haines. She had been quieter than usual today and Dil did not consider that a bad quality for a woman. Despite her unglamorous get-up he suddenly found her unbearably appealing.

"I'd been plannin' on it," he said. "But I guess if you

don't mind I better stick around a day or two and see if I can find any of your stock them varmints run off."

Hallie glanced anxiously at her mother. Miz Haines seemed to be undergoing some inner crisis. "I sure would be obliged," she finally said. And for the first time this day Miss Hallie almost smiled.

Dil finished his coffee and stood. "Which way you suppose they went?" he asked, then realized that they could have gone only one of two ways: upcreek or down. And he had just come from upcreek. He picked up his rifle by the door and mounted old Bill.

He found the first horse less than half a mile down the road, grazing in a boggy flat. After a moment's thought he guessed that there would be more time saved if instead of leaving it to look for the rest he were to bring the horse back to the house so that Hallie could ride too.

Miz Haines was plainly worried as her daughter rode off into the woods with this stranger but apparently she decided that she had little choice. As they rode down the creek road Dil suggested, "You ride the right bank as far away from the road as you can without gettin' lost and I'll take the left."

"Why can't we go together?" the girl asked.

"Because this way we'll cover twice as much ground and get the job done faster." It seemed an eminently practical suggestion to Dil and he couldn't figure out why Miss Hallie seemed so put out as she splashed her horse through the foot-deep water. "You give me a whoop and a holler every once in a while," he called after her. It was impossible to tell if she had heard.

A couple of miles closer to town Dil found another horse and a couple of hundred yards past that he saw the cow, her udder nearly as swollen as the last time he had found her. She moaned a plaintive greeting as she saw him. "Miss Hallie," he yelled, "I found your critter." He called several more times before he realized that the girl was not going to answer.

He remembered her annoyed manner as she had ridden off alone into the jackpines. Women, he guessed, were more annoyingly unpredictable than horses. And Dil had never regarded the horse as one of God's more gifted creatures. He sighed and began leading the cow and horse back to the Haines house.

"Where's Hallie?" Miz Haines asked sharply.

Dil shrugged. "Off ridin' t'other side of the creek, I guess. I yelled and she wouldn't answer." Suddenly he was infected with Miz Haines' worry. "I'll go see," he promised, and dug his heels into old Bill until the Chunk broke into a lumbering trot.

Splashing across the creek, he followed her horse's tracks. He wondered if this side of the valley was swampy or entangled with blackberry vines or just what had made her so unwilling to tackle it alone. Then a vague suspicion began growing in him. "Naw," he told himself. She couldn't have been mad just because she wanted to ride along with him. Maybe she was really afraid of something.

But what? Whoever had run off the Haines' horses and critter had done his deviltry yesterday, probably at the same time that he had doctored up Dil's stove. There he went, thinking of it as *his* stove again. He followed her horse's heavy hoofprints through the soft, damp ground beneath the trees, then suddenly realized that there was something wrong.

There was a muddle of prancing hoofprints. From two directions the small prints of unshod riding stock had converged on the larger ones of Miss Hallie's plow horse. From the melee the three prints merged into one trail as the horses climbed up over the mountain. They had a head start and even Miss Hallie's plow horse was younger, lighter, and faster than old Bill. Dill stared after the footprints heading straight toward the reservation. Now what, he wondered, was he going to do? Withal, he felt a vague resentment at the girl's way of disappearing. She could at least have yelled and raised a fuss, he thought.

CHAPTER 10

When he rode back Miz Haines didn't have to ask. They stared at each other for a moment in mute despair. Dil pondered. The smart thing for him to do would be to go in to town and raise hell until that scholarly-looking little sheriff with the pince-nez glasses got off the dime and did something. Remembering the eager mob in the hotel bar, Dil suspected that it would be somewhat easier to prod the sheriff into action now that a woman was involved. But if he went in to town the trail would be cold.

"Can you ride?" he asked Miz Haines.

"I'm gettin' kind of stiff for it," she said, "but I guess I can if I have to."

He looked over the horse he had just brought back. It was younger and smaller than old Bill. He glanced down at his rifle. "You got any better gun you could spare me?"

Miz Haines thought for a moment. "Al left me an old pair of Colts," she said. "I'll give you one and I'll take the other into town. You want anything else?"

Dil thought for a moment. "Some blankets and something to eat," he suggested. Sliding off of old Bill, he tied the horse's reins to the pump handle. While he rummaged in the barn and found a bridle and a scarred old saddle Miz Haines was busy in the house. She emerged as he was leading the smaller horse from the barn. "When you get to town," he said, "tell 'em it was two men ridin' unshod. Headin' for the reservation."

Miz Haines handed him one of the pistols. Strapping

the other around her ample waist, she looked up at Dil. "You still think them Indians are honest?" she asked. Dil was very thoughtful as he splashed across the creek again and began following the three sets of hoofprints up the mountain. "But goldang it," he muttered, "she could've yelled or somethin'!"

The tracks went for nearly a mile up a forty-five-degree slope. When he finally reached the top Dil stopped to blow his horse. He examined the venerable Colt Miz Haines had loaned him. He unloaded it and familiarized himself with the action, drawing it and snapping the hammer against trees and whatnot until he guessed that he stood a faint chance of hitting something. But if it came to that kind of range he could just as well throw rocks, he guessed. Sighing, Dil hoped that Miss Hallie would have sense enough to delay her captors as much as possible. It stood to reason that three people traveling together would move more slowly than one. If he could just get within picking-off range before they saw him, maybe the 45-90 would take care of at least one of the men before they went to ground, providing that they didn't stay so bunched up his shooting would endanger Miss Hallie.

His horse snorted and bent its neck to crop at sparse timberline grass. Dil glanced over the endless undulations of mountain, glancing back toward Winville, then ahead toward the reservation. He hoped the trail would remain easy to follow. He clucked and dug his unspurred heels into the horse. He still had twelve cartridges for the 45-90. Miz Haines had given him a handful for the Colt. As the horse started down the other side of the mountain, forcing him forward into the saddle, Dil suddenly realized that by nightfall he was going to have a brand-new set of blisters. He began counting bullets and putting them in separate pockets.

Abruptly he was crossing an outcropping of slippery

rock so steep that his horse slipped and struggled to gain a foothold. He looked ahead. The apron of smooth rock extended a couple of hundred yards before there was soil again. Gritting his teeth, he forced the horse straight across. When he reached the other side there were no tracks. He first cut right, then left along the rock apron, looking for renewed tracks. There were none. Uphill the rock became gradually steeper until no horse could make it. Downhill . . .

He began making his way around the lower edge of the rock apron, struggling through gnarled timberline trees broader than they were high. Finally he found the new set of tracks, exiting on the same side as they had come in.

Dil studied the countryside, scratching his head. They weren't heading for the reservation unless there was some secret cleft in the hills that had to be totally invisible from this vantage point. The tracks were angling back downhill into the lower canyon of Bear Creek but it seemed as if the two strangers were planning to come out considerably above the Haines place.

Suddenly Dil knew exactly where they planned to come out. With a sudden sick feeling he knew exactly what they were planning. After they had done whatever it was that that kind of men felt like doing to Miss Hallie they would butcher her. But not just anywhere. Dil knew that by the time he could go for help they would have bloodied his lean-to, his clothes, everything he owned in an effort to make sure that if they couldn't kill him with their own bullets the outraged townspeople would do it with ropes.

He closed his eyes in silent prayer, whipped the loose end of a rope over the horse's rump, and hung on to the horn with one hand, praying that he would not lose his grip on the rifle with the other. The horse took a tentative step down the steep hillside, then looked back plaintively. Dil slapped the rope down again, hard. The horse moved out.

He whipped it repeatedly and soon the horse was galloping downhill, taking great twenty-yard leaps and skids down the mountainside, running frantically to keep from falling down.

Dil lay low over the saddle, trying to dodge whipping branches, struggling to stay in the saddle with one frantic, leather-clawing hand while he gripped the 45-90 with the other. Finally, an eternity later, they had reached the bottom and were splashing across Bear Creek. If he stopped to let the horse blow it might go into a sulk and never move again. Slapping frantically with the rope end, he lashed the horse into a wild runaway gallop up the Bear Creek road toward his lean-to.

He wanted to yell and whistle at the horse but he was making enough noise now to wake the dead. He wondered if the strangers were proceeding with due caution. Probably not. Their false trail had been pretty neat. Besides . . . it was due only to luck that he and Miz Haines had not wasted several hours more in chasing down stock before they began to wonder about Hallie. If Dil had guessed right they would be plowing through the trees, making as much noise as he was. He wondered if he could make it to his lean-to before they did.

Near's he could work it out, they ought to arrive about the same time. He glanced at the sky but the snow clouds lay solid in every direction and he had no idea what time it was. Goldang it, he told himself, she wanted to ride with me! Why didn't I let her? If they kill her now—or if they . . . No matter what they did to Hallie he knew that he would be blamed for it. And the hell of it was, he knew that he would be partly to blame. They had tried to kill him three times. They had gotten Hallie's father. Why hadn't he had sense enough to realize that they weren't through yet?

He was a mile from home before the horse began slowing and remained adamant to any further persuasion with the rope end. He guessed that if he was to have any horse left he'd better cool it out for the last mile.

It was another quarter mile before the horse stopped blowing and he was afforded an occasional chance to listen for other noise between the beast's shuddering breaths. Once he thought that he heard the jingle of a bit but no matter how he listened it didn't come again. He guessed that he must have imagined it.

The lean-to was still there. From the road he saw no horses or other sign. Had they been there already? Were they hiding in case he showed up? Maybe they had been listening to the infernal racket his horse had been making. Maybe Miss Hallie was already . . . He forced himself not to think about it.

The horse was so weary that it was starting to stumble. Dil slipped out of the saddle and ground-tied the horse. He began sneaking up on his own lean-to, listening for something—anything. If only he weren't panting so bad. He struggled to slow down his breathing and his racing pulse. It was no use. He had circled around now until he was on the hillside above the lean-to—where he had hidden out this morning when Joe Spokane and the other two Indians had arrived.

The lean-to was silent. No sign or smell of horses either. Abruptly he was assailed with the horrible suspicion that he had guessed wrong. Maybe they weren't coming this way at all! He wondered if the second set of tracks he had discovered had been a double feint. Maybe they were heading off downtown, paralleling the road as he and Hallie had done when hunting stock. He sighed and breathed the sour smell of fear and sweat and defeat. Growing in him was the visceral certainty that he would never again see Miss Hallie alive. He wondered how old she was. Sixteen, maybe seventeen? Far too young for a man of twenty-three to be thinking about that way, even if he had possessed some prospects of ever being able to support a wife. He wondered momentarily if Papa had perhaps felt this way when he had seen whatever it was closing in on him up somewhere in the Klondike.

He was slowly melting into a puddle of defeat and despair when he heard it. Somewhere behind and to one side a bridle jingled. He suddenly realized that he had not even checked his rifle since the mad dash downhill. He ran a hand over it. Sights seemed unbattered. The action worked smoothly. It was loaded. He drew the Colt. Everything ready.

Moments later he saw the trio of horses moving obliquely down the hillside, heading for his lean-to. The slim, bib-overalled figure in the middle had a feedbag over its head, looking at this distance very like the hood that Dil had always heard about but never seen at a public hanging. From the awkward, hunched posture he suddenly realized that Hallie had both hands tied to the horns of her plow horse's hames.

If they continued on their present course they would pass within twenty yards of him, Dil knew. He eased back the hammer on the 45-90 and tried to make up his mind whether to shoot the one in front or the one in back. For an instant he toyed with the idea of confronting them with the business end of a rifle and taking them both alive. But Dil knew that he couldn't hope ever to get off two shots quick enough if they were warned. If he could nail one of them without warning—the way they had repeatedly tried to do him in—at least it would even up the odds somewhat.

Would they retreat or plunge forward up the creek? If they knew the country upstream they would know it was a cul-de-sac. He began drawing a bead on the rearmost horseman, then realized that the one in front would be holding

Hallie's lead rope. He switched his aim to the man in front. They were close now—an easy shot. This time he felt no compunctions about bushwhacking a stranger. After all, the sons of bitches had Hallie, didn't they? He began squeezing the trigger.

The 45-90 roared like a small cannon, echoes reverberating from the mountains, and Dil saw the lead horseman propelled sideways as if by a sledgehammer. His horse reared and emitted a shrill scream. He was jacking a second shell into the rifle as the rearmost horseman spurred past Hallie, grabbed her lead rope, and began moving leisurely toward Dil's lean-to, keeping himself directly ahead of her with easy accuracy.

Gritting his teeth with frustrated rage, Dil trained his smoking rifle on tantalizing bits of hat and jacket that protruded momentarily from behind Miss Hallie's bound and hooded form. For a long-enough-to-shoot instant the other horse's rump was exposed but before Dil could bring himself to injure the blameless animal it was shielded once more by Hallie's horse. He was still cursing himself for this singular inability to make up his mind when the ill-matched pair rode off past his lean-to, heading out onto the Bear Creek road.

Dil got to his feet and began moving down the hillside. He approached the fallen man cautiously. The stranger didn't move. He wore a mackinaw and a stocking cap against the chill weather but when Dil rolled him over he saw that it was one of the men who had worn a four-cornered engineer's hat the other day. He was pretty sure that it was the one who had lain for him the day he was going after the bull elk—the game warden.

One thing was sure, Dil guessed. Now the man they called Groby would never have another chance to get even for the way Dil had creased him with a 45-90 slug.

He began trotting back to the road where he had ground-tied his horse.

Then abruptly he realized that the other man was leading Hallie's horse upstream toward the falls. If he continued that way he would be trapped. All Dil had to do was wait for Miz Haines to bring reinforcements. He went back to the dead game warden and began rummaging through his pockets.

The man had a .38 pistol, which was lighter and, Dil suspected, probably more accurate than the venerable Colt loaned to him. Apart from that his pockets produced nothing but the usual clutter of cigar clipper, cigars, matches, jackknife, a silver dollar, and seventy-eight cents in miscellaneous change. No matter how he searched Dil could find no billfold, no identifying document, no badge or anything to indicate who or what Groby had really been. He wondered momentarily why the man had not carried a rifle.

Finally Dil relieved the corpse of the .38, along with belt and holster. It didn't match the Colt and the holster hung butt-forward when he put it on his left side but Dil guessed that he was finally and maybe just barely the kind of two-gun man he had read about in dime novels. He gave the dead man a final kick and began moving down to his horse.

He guessed that he should have known better than to ground-tie old Bill in strange country but . . . goldang it! If something went wrong out here he wouldn't feel right dying with old Bill tied solid where he'd perish miserably and end up feeding coyotes. It was bad enough men had to die that way.

CHAPTER 11

Dil gazed despairingly skyward, wondering if there was anything else he could possibly do wrong. It would take him a couple of hours to walk to the Haines place. Then he realized that there were no more horses there. He wondered if Miz Haines had made it to town by now. And if she had, how long would it take her to prod some life into that lethargic sheriff and get some reinforcements out here? Dil guessed that there was nothing else for it. He would have to follow them on foot.

Sooner or later Hallie's captor would realize that he was heading into a blind alley. Then he would be faced with the choice of holing up or trying to fight his way back down. The smart thing to do would be to wait. But . . . Dil remembered how attractive Miss Hallie had managed to be even in bib overalls several sizes too large. He knew that if the man who held her ever got time to stop and rest, to look at Hallie . . . Dil checked his rifle and his pair of mismatched pistols. Nobody could say he didn't have enough guns or ammunition. He started walking up the Bear Creek road, following fresh tracks in the damp, sandy soil.

For the first mile it was easy. Then he reached the end of the road and had to follow the trail through clumps of sumac, lodgepole, spruce, and jackpine as he struggled to penetrate the ever-narrowing gorge. He tried to remember the country from the morning he had hunted old Bill up here. What would it be like, he wondered, to be possessed of the photographic memory every dime-novel cowboy or Indian seemed to possess? Dil studied the increasingly vertical terrain, trying to remember. Surely it couldn't be more than another couple of miles before the canyon narrowed to nothing and Bear Creek became a waterfall. He slowed, following the tracks with difficulty over the slabs of smooth stone, wondering how far ahead they were or if Hallie's abductor was doubling back to draw a bead on him.

He wanted to shy away from the path and poke along under cover of the thick undergrowth but if he did he would lose the track. The creek was rushing and babbling so loudly here that he could not have heard a whole troop of cavalry.

But he did manage to hear the shot that went past him and spattered lead on the stratified rock behind him. Instantly he leaped to one side, analyzing the direction from which the shot had come and diving into the best cover available. It was drying sumac and almost immediately he began sneezing. He gave silent thanks for the rush of Bear Creek, which was louder than the noise he was making. Another shot clipped the bush over his head.

He was pinned down. But good. Unless he could get out of here and find out exactly where the other man was shooting from, Dil knew, it made no difference whether he had three guns or three dozen. He wondered which he had the most ammunition for and decided that the full bandolier that went with the dead game warden's gun was the logical candidate. He was getting ready to fire a few shots at random just to slow down the other man when abruptly he realized that Hallie was out there somewhere. Looking straight up, he asked, "Goldang it! Whose side are you on?"

He supposed he ought to be praying, but damn it all! Abruptly he realized an idea that must have slowly been maturing ever since Papa had failed to come home and Mama had died: If the God they had always tried to tell him about in Sunday school was all-powerful and knew everything, then why the hell was he out here pinned down without a horse and someone was up there gettin' ready to do just whatever he wanted to with Miss Hallie? He looked straight up again. "You son of a bitch!" he growled. "Just wait till I get them other bastards!"

Another shot clipped the dry sumac overhead, making so little disturbance that he almost didn't notice it over the rush of water. But he did see it and he noted that it came from a slightly different angle. For a moment he thought that he was surrounded, then realized that while he was pinned down the stranger was working his way around, back downstream. If Dil didn't do something soon he would be left out here, some twenty miles from town and afoot.

He began creeping downstream through the brush. The other man couldn't possibly be seeing him or, Dil knew, he would have been dead by now. The trouble was, the other man could shoot any- and everywhere, not caring whom he killed. Dil didn't dare shoot blind—not if he ever hoped to see Hallie alive again. Something—it looked like drifting ashes—was coming down. Dil rubbed his eyes and groaned. It was starting to snow.

Another bullet sang overhead and he was far enough from the rushing creek to hear it. But the echoes in this narrow canyon were so confusing that he couldn't tell which direction it came from. He found a pine cone and tossed it back toward where he had been a moment ago. This time he saw the direction of the answering shot. The man was already ahead of him, moving back downstream. He thought irrelevantly of the three sticks of blasting powder still hidden on the hillside above his lean-to. If only it weren't for Hallie he would be happy to toss them about in the same prodigal way that this man was wasting bullets.

He began creeping downstream, trying to parallel the other. It didn't make sense that he couldn't move quieter and faster than a man encumbered with two horses and a girl captive yet the next shot overhead came from still farther downstream. Dil stood and began moving in a running crouch, expecting a slug through his hunched backbone at any instant. But by now the other man was shooting wildly, merely spraying the canyon with bullets to slow Dil down.

Dil had moved, he guessed, close to half a mile and the creek was running quieter now before he dared stand full height and try to see the other man. Suddenly he stumbled on the trail again and saw hoofprints overlaying the previous three sets, this time heading downstream. He broke into a run, then remembered how the tracks had doubled back once before. Gritting his teeth with rage and impatience, he went back into the tangle of brush paralleling the creek and began fighting his way back downstream.

Occasionally he stood still to listen for the sound of hooves or the jingle of bits. The creek was still making too much noise. A lone whiskey jack flew overhead, shrieking its territorial imperative, and he could scarcely hear the shrill call.

There was nothing else for it. He shouldered his way through the brittle sumac, hoping that the rushing creek would cover his noise as thoroughly as it was concealing the other man's.

It was hopeless. There might be men who could track an opponent and even outflank him under these circumstances but Dil knew that he was blundering blindly through the brush, accomplishing nothing. He kept ploughing downstream, making as much noise as a herd of feeding elephants. Slowly the ground leveled out and the overwhelming noise of rushing water lessened. He thought he heard a voice once, then the creak of leather and jingle of a bit. It wasn't too far ahead. He eased out into the path and tried to move faster. It couldn't be too much farther, he knew, to the roadhead.

He was within yards of the roadhead when he heard the sound of an automobile being cranked. He broke cover and began running. He got there just in time to see a Dodge with its top up disappearing down the road toward Winville.

Dil stood for a moment, raging, feeling even greater anger as he realized how ridiculous he looked with a rifle and a pair of mismatched pistols. Then abruptly he realized that if the stranger had made his getaway with a car then his and Miss Hallie's horses had to be somewhere around here. He began looking for them.

The stranger, he guessed, had done a first-class job of running them off. He quartered back and forth across the narrow canyon without finding so much as a track. Jays and whiskey jacks chronicled his movements. Once a crow cawed, but he could not find the horses. Then he heard the sound of another automobile.

Dil listened. He didn't know all that much about cars but this seemed the loudest he had heard in some time. Finally he realized that it wasn't just one car. While he listened the first car stopped. Moments later two more arrived. "You boys take that side," somebody called. A gun went off.

"See him?" another voice called.

Oh, Jesus! Dil thought. Within minutes the woods would be full of them, happily slaughtering one another, shooting at everything that breathed or crawled, annihilating every piece of foliage unfortunate enough to be moved by the wind or one another. City hunters, he supposed. Then he knew who they really were. Miz Haines had finally made it to town and now the good citizens of Winville were bringing law and order to Bear Creek.

He found a piece of flat rock exposed by Bear Creek's spring flooding. He threw it mightily downstream. After the twelfth shot he lost count. Dil wholeheartedly wished he were somewhere else.

"See him?" somebody asked again.

"Thought I did for a minute," somebody called back. There was an abrupt fusillade again. This time none of the bullets came near Dil.

"Goddamnit, stop that!" a voice yelled. "You're shootin' at me!"

"Why don't you all stop it for a minute?" Dil called. "They got away ten minutes ago."

"Who's that?"

"Dil Reeves. If you'll all just stop shootin' like city hunters I'll come out of my hole and show you which way they went."

Finally, after more minutes of senseless wrangling, the citizens of Bear Creek were gathered together at the road-head and listening to Dil. He recognized some of them from the day in the saloon after Al Haines' funeral. He looked around the group. "Where's Miz Haines?" he asked, and learned that she was home taking care of her stock.

"Didn't any of you see a Dodge tearin' down the road when you were coming out here?" Dil asked.

Nobody had. Which meant that the car had somehow dodged into one of the branches leading to a ranch—possibly the entrance to Dil's own lean-to—until the pack had passed, and now the man who had Miss Hallie could be anywhere—maybe heading out the opposite end of Win-ville. Dil felt like crying. Instead he repeated several heart-felt phrases not learned at his mother's knee. "At least I got one of them," he concluded.

"Who?" It was a man who had bought him a drink the other day.

"Can't swear to it," Dil said. "Maybe you all could have a look at him."

"How many was there?"

So, by fits and starts, Dil found himself telling the whole story of Miss Hallie's abduction, jumping back and forth erratically to fill in details. Meanwhile he was leading them back down the road toward his lean-to. It would be there, he supposed, that he would find Miss Hallie's abductor—there had to be another one, he suddenly realized, unless that high-topped Dodge had driven out here by itself.

"Miz Haines said it was Injuns."

"Nope," Dil said. "I saw 'em. And they were both white." He was hurrying down the road though he knew it was useless. Anybody smart enough to anticipate this motorized rabble of vigilantes would be too smart to linger around Dil's lean-to. Then he was stricken with a sudden suspicion. Anybody that smart at doubling back . . .

He studied the faces around him. They were vaguely familiar, he guessed from that day in town when they had assembled to bury Al Haines. He studied the cars. Two flivvers and a Star. No sign of a Dodge. "Another good idea shot to hell," he muttered.

"What were you thinking?" It was the man who had bought him a drink.

"Though he might have ditched Miss Hallie somewhere in the brush and joined up with you."

"And?"

Dil shook his head. "You people all live out on Bear Creek?" he asked.

There was general agreement.

"You know three city-slicker types in a flivver, with four-cornered hats and surveyin' tools?"

Several of the Bear Creekers had seen them but Dil learned nothing he had not known already. He wondered about the man he had just killed. Groby, who called himself a game warden, of whom nobody seemed overly fond—not even the apathetic sheriff down in Winville.

It just didn't make sense for a lawman—even if he was only a game warden . . . Somehow Dil could not imagine any kind of lawman being so openly and blatantly disregardful of the legalities. He wondered if it was a case of mistaken identity. Who had told him that this man was Groby? Who had told him that Groby was game warden? He sighed and continued walking down the road. Finally half of the Bear Creekers detached themselves from the party and went back to the cars. He was nearing the entrance to his own place when he heard the two flivvers and a Star grinding down the rutted incline. They caught up just as he was entering his own turn-off.

The lean-to seemed the same as he had left it. But so far there had been no sign of old Bill or any of the other horses. That, he supposed, would take another day or two. He had to find his horse before he could do anything effective about Miss Hallie. Lord Almighty! Couldn't anything go right?

He consoled himself with the thought that at least some of these men would be able to accurately identify the man he had shot. And if the man was known they ought to be able to apply enough moral pressure on that useless old dotard of a sheriff to make him round up the man's associates. It wasn't until Dil had led the makeshift posse past his lean-to and up to the hillside where he had scragged one of Miss Hallie's captors that he realized that even this scant hope was gone. There was no body. No matter how he searched it was as if he had never killed anybody. The man he had shot was just plain gone!

CHAPTER 12

Dil stood nonplussed for a moment. He could sense that some of these Bear Creekers were beginning to suspect he had never shot anyone at all. Then he was filled with sudden desperate inspiration. "This belt and gun," he said. "Anybody know whose it is? I took it off the man I shot."

Men handled the .38, passing it down the line. There were opinions. There were guesses. There were increasingly wild conjectures and finally Dil knew that nobody recognized the gun. He took it back and buckled it around his waist again.

"Anybody see any horses running around loose as you came up the road?" he finally remembered to ask.

Nobody had.

Dil decided that there was nothing else he could do out here. He got into the Star with the man who had bought him a drink and they began bouncing the sixteen rutted miles back in to town. He supposed the sheriff would be just as ignorant of whose gun he had appropriated as all these blundering, well-meaning men. He remembered the three pepper-and-salt-suited Indians and wondered how they fitted into it.

"Anybody ever try to get you off your place?" he asked the man who drove the Star. "By the way, where do you live?"

"I'm Joe Hagen, next place downstream from Al Haines," the man said. "Nope, nobody tried to run me off but I found some strangers diggin' holes along my stretch of creekbank. I damn sure run *them* off!"

"You heard anything about hydraulickers?"

Hagen shook his head.

Dil told him what he had learned from Joe Spokane and the other Indians. "They'd like to get together with us," he added. "But nobody here seems t'care much for Indians. There been some trouble?"

Joe Hagen shook his head again. "Nothin' much," he said over the rattle and cough of the Star. "People always like to blame somebody else when stock goes astray."

Though the sandy ruts ran mainly downhill the Star began steaming. Hagen reluctantly pulled to one side and the flivvers passed, raising a tremendous cloud of dust. They got water from the creek and quenched the thirsty radiator. There was still dust in the air as they once more began lurching down the road to Winville.

"Mind if we stop at Miz Haines'?" Dil asked.

"Might as well. Give this dust time to settle."

Miz Haines was worn and drawn, her ample figure beginning to show a long-hidden angularity. When Dil shook his head her expression did not change. They stood, awkward, not knowing what to say to one another. Finally Dil remembered that he was still wearing one of Al Haines' pistols. He took it off and handed it to her. She looked at the smaller pistol he was wearing. Dil told her where he had gotten it. Miz Haines inspected the .38 and shook her head. There was another awkward silence and then Dil was bouncing along the rutted road once more. Gradually the snow turned into rain. He cranked the windshield wiper while Hagen struggled with the slippery ruts. Finally they were at the entrance to Hagen's place.

The Star stopped at the gateway. "My old woman's feelin' poorly," Hagen said. Obviously he was embarrassed at what he had to do. "I got to feed the stock and take care of the milkin' and cut a little wood. Maybe if you'd like to spend the night I could run you into town in the morning."

Dil sighed. He knew that he ought to feel outraged but . . . Hagen had his own problems just as everybody else did. He couldn't let his place go to hell just because somebody had kidnapped a neighbor's girl. Before he could ask the next question Hagen added, "My horses are all off somewhere in the woods. Take a day or two to find them."

"Yeah. Well, thanks for the ride," Dil said. He got out of the car and began slogging through the rain toward Winville. He couldn't remember whether it was eight or ten miles from here.

Water began trickling down his collar. The 45-90 was going to have to be taken apart and oiled once he got under cover. Somehow it seemed to have gained weight in the last mile or two. It turned dark and he began stumbling as the rain turned slowly into sleet and the ruts became more treacherous in the darkness. He didn't know what time it was. He seemed to be losing all contact with reality as he slogged numbly down the road.

He had to do something about Miss Hallie. But what could he do? Whoever got her had gotten away clean. And the Bear Creekers had seen no loose horses. Which meant that old Bill and the other two were probably dead somewhere deep in the brush. He was helpless now —unable to do anything for Hallie, unable even to do anything for himself. The only way he was going to survive this winter without starving or freezing to death was by taking that apathetic little man's offer of a job as deputy.

Slogging through the wet and constantly colder night, he remembered the sheriff's sweltering office with nostalgia. A warm place to pull off his boots, a square meal, a cup of coffee . . . He felt guilt at the precedence these simple needs were taking over Miss Hallie's predicament. He wondered where she was at the moment. Dead? He tried to remind himself that if they had wanted her dead they could have killed her much earlier and with less trouble. He hoped that they still had her with them, somewhere warm. Mostly he hoped that she had not turned into an embarrassment to her captors–into something better left bound and blindfolded to freeze to death and be obliterated by coyotes and other varmints.

He passed the ford, not even feeling the cold water over his numbed feet. Nellie's legs still pointed grotesquely skyward but he could see that the varmints had already been at her. If he didn't get into town soon and get his feet warm there was a fair chance that the varmints would be feeding off Dil too, he suddenly realized.

Finally he saw the outskirts of Winville. Plodding awkwardly on numb feet in frozen boots, he made it to the sheriff's office. Locked. So was the Mercantile. He struggled on to the hotel.

The barman looked askance when he stumped into the saloon burdened with rifle and pistol but relaxed when Dil propped the rifle in a corner and fell into a chair next to the stove. "Cold outside?" he asked.

Dil nodded.

The barman poured whiskey.

"I ain't got no money," Dil warned. "And besides I don't much care for whiskey anyway."

The barman laughed and poured the whiskey back into the bottle. "Can't stand it myself," he confessed. "Like a cup of coffee?"

Dil reckoned he would. "Seen the sheriff?" he asked when he had stanched the sudden flow of mucus elicited by hot coffee.

The barman shook his head. "I heard there was some trouble up north county in the mines. Anyhow, last I knew the little giant was packing a grip and hotfootin' it up there."

"He take a train or somethin'?"

The barman shook his head. "Ford."

Dil warmed up enough to start shivering uncontrollably. "D-didn't anybody t-tell him what h-happened out on B-bear C-c-creek?"

"Thought I recognized you!" the barman said suddenly. "You're that young feller everybody wanted to stand a drink to t'other day."

Dil drew a deep breath and held it, struggling momentarily to control his shivering. "Did the sheriff know about the kidnapping?" he repeated.

The barman shrugged. "S'pose he did. But you can't expect him to go chasin' around after some homesteader's daughter when the mine owners are havin' labor troubles."

Dil guessed that he couldn't. Someday, though, he decided, he was going to kill that poor excuse for a sheriff—after he had kicked his butt publicly up and down the single dusty street of Winville. But first, like it or not, he had to take the job that the scholarly-appearing little man in the sheepskin vest had dangled in front of him. And even before that he had to figure out where he was going to spend tonight.

"How much is a room?" he asked.

"Dollar."

That settled that. Dil endured another bout of shivering. When it was over he drew the .38 and extended it butt first to the barman.

"You want to sell it or just hock it?"

Dil shrugged. There was a moment of awkward silence as they stared at each other. "Sheriff offered me a job as deputy," he finally added.

The barman relaxed. "You'll be needin' the gun," he said. "Maybe I can—" He broke off as a portly man in blue serge stepped into the barroom and stopped in shocked disbelief at the sight of the pistol. The barman finished handing it back to Dil, who holstered it. "Guess I can't either," the barman muttered. "That's the boss." Raising his voice, he added, "Why don't you try the livery stable?"

Dil nodded curtly and stalked out of the bar. He had not realized how exhausted he was until he tried to walk again. His boots were still stiff from the soaking and he moved drunkenly down the street. Then he realized what the barman had been trying to tell him. He doubled back down the alley and found the stable behind the hotel. There was no watchman–nothing apart from the couple of cows kept for milk and a horse even older and more placidly bovine than the cows. Dil burrowed into the hay piled at one end of the stable and tried to shiver himself to sleep.

He had always heard that men about to freeze to death became sleepy and that their final departure was actually pleasant. If that was true then he wasn't going to die, for Dil could not remember when he had ever been colder, more miserable and discouraged, more willing to give up and die.

He thought back to Miz Haines' bleak face and suddenly a new doubt assailed him. She was a woman alone in the woods, newly widowed, and now her daughter had just disappeared in company with Dil, a stranger who had caused her husband's death. He wondered what he would have thought if he'd been in her shoes.

Was it fear or just a Quaker conscience that had kept her from turning the Colt onto him the instant he had returned it to her? "Goldang it!" he muttered to the cows and the ancient horse, "if that sheriff don't get back early tomorrow I'm gonna be in one fine fix!" He succumbed to another paroxysm of shivering.

The horse was making rasping noises, licking at something. Abruptly Dil realized what it was. He crawled out of the hay and sidled past the aged horse to the manger. There was still half a handful of oats caught in the corners of the box where the horse's tongue couldn't reach. Scrabbling in the darkness with his fingernails, Dil captured a mouthful. He got as much as he could hold in his hands, then retired once more to his bed in the hay and lay chewing, chewing, trying to grind the hard hulled oats down fine enough to extract some nourishment. After a while he felt the numbness start to leave his feet. Before he had finished his careful chewing of oats his feet were throbbing with the painful aftermath of frostbite.

Morning dawned clear and sunny. It took Dil several dazed minutes to remember where he was and to realize that he was not dead, that he had actually managed to sleep. He yawned and stretched, thankful to be young and alive. The horse did not seem at all put out from having been forced to share his oats with Dil.

Then abruptly Dil was wide awake again and he realized that nothing had really changed from last night except that he was a day older and Miss Hallie had been in strange hands a day longer. He cringed mentally at the thought of what might be happening to her and wondered if there was really a fate worse than death. Would Miss Hallie want to die if she ever escaped? He wondered what Miz Haines would feel. Then he was sobered at the realization that none of them would have much choice. If the villains were who he thought they were, they had everything to gain with a silent and dead girl.

He remembered some of the dead faces he had seen in his brief lifetime—how an undertaker had managed to turn his mother into some painted caricature whose face had shocked him more deeply than the simple fact of her merciful death. Somewhere now maybe the varmints were gnawing on Miss Hallie.

He tried to put it from his mind and reminded himself of what he had to do if he was to survive long enough to avenge Miss Hallie and her father. He was going to have to eat humble pie with that scholarly-looking, pince-nezed sheriff. There wasn't the slightest chance in hell of ever getting the old man off the dime, but maybe with a badge on, maybe with a square meal inside him, he could squeeze some information out of somebody. He wondered if the sheriff was back yet from his strike-breaking up at the mines.

There was only one way to find out. Dil brushed the hayseed out of his hair and strode from the stable. The sun was actually warm this morning, raising steamy wisps from puddles on Winville's main street. As it warmed his back Dil felt better. He was still alive in spite of all their efforts to the contrary. The sheriff had offered him money and a badge. Surely with this kind of backing he could go out and find– Suddenly remembering that Miss Hallie was somewhere, in somebody else's hands, he didn't feel happy at all.

CHAPTER 13

He clumped down the street to the sheriff's office, wet boots thumping awkwardly on the loose planking of the sidewalk. When he got there the sheriff's office was open. Thanking God for small favors, he went in.

This time there was no roaring fire. The office was comfortable. A strange young man no older than Dil looked up from the *Spokesman Review*. "What can I do for you?" he asked.

"I, uh—I come t'see the sheriff," Dil said.

"Ain't here. I'm the deputy."

Dil stared at the young man in silent consternation. Then he remembered that Al Haines had told him there was one deputy. "Uh—you expect him back soon?"

The deputy shrugged. They stared at each other for a silent moment which ended when the telephone rang. The deputy got out of his chair and went to the wall. He took the receiver off the hook and banged it several times. "Sorry, Sarah," he shouted. "Can't hear a thing. You want-a try it again?"

There were several moments of silence while the operator tried for a better connection. Finally the deputy was speaking again. "Yes, sir, I hear you now all right. Yes, sir. No. Oh!" Suddenly there was genuine shock in his voice. "When'd it happen? Yeah, uh—yes, sir. Yes, sir. Thank you. Good-bye." Dazedly the deputy hung up. He returned to his chair and sat before looking up at Dil as if suddenly remembering him. "Sheriff ain't ever comin' back," he explained. "You got any business, you might's well tell me."

"What happened?"

"The old man died."

"Died?" Dil echoed.

"Heart finally give out on him. Mr. Richardson, he's the mine manager, says he went in his sleep last night."

Dil faced the crushed remnant of his hopes. When he had time to sort out his feelings he would be able to admit that he felt not the slightest pain at the death of the useless and obstructive old man. But why did he have to die just now—just after he'd promised Dil a job?

"Anything I can do for you?" the deputy asked. Already he was shuffling papers and sitting more possessively in the old man's chair.

"Nope," Dil said and stalked back out into the late October sunlight. "Now just where," he asked himself, "do I go from here?"

The oats he had stolen from an aged horse last night were doing vile things to his digestive system. He stood on the boardwalk in front of the sheriff's office, teetering on his sore feet, trying to decide what to do. It was a long walk back to Miz Haines' and he hated to arrive empty-handed, but . . . if he didn't get something to eat soon he was going to be in such bad shape. . . .

Abruptly he remembered the pistol. It looked nice to have a gun at his belt but it was also faintly ridiculous now that he was not going to be a deputy after all, and he knew he couldn't outdraw anybody or hit anything if he did somehow manage to get it out of the holster without shooting off a couple of toes. He glanced up and down the street and found the three gilded balls.

It was another half hour before the proprietor came from the rear of the shop and glanced fearfully at the man who squatted hunkered down in his doorway with a 45-90 rifle between his legs and a pistol at his waist. Dil drew the pistol and held it out butt foremost. The small, dark-bearded man in the shop still hesitated until Dil broke the weapon and put the cartridges in his pocket. He did the same with the rifle and the pawnkeeper unbolted the door.

"How much?" Dil asked.

"Both of them?"

"No, I want to keep the rifle."

The small man examined the pistol, peering down the barrel toward sunlight that came through the shop front. "Ten dollars," he said.

"How much for the belt, holster, ammunition?"

"Ten dollars for everything."

Dil's stomach churned and his mouth watered at the thought of what just twenty-five cents worth of breakfast could do to re-establish him among the living. The pistol had cost him nothing—apart from a stranger's life and just possibly Miss Hallie's. He buckled the holster back on. The pawnbroker stared doubtfully at him. Silently Dil reloaded the pistol and stalked out of the shop.

"Fifteen," the small man called after him.

Dil kept walking.

"I'll give you twenty."

Dil intended to stalk angrily onward. But his body had already rebelled, thinking hungrily of breakfast, of a new pair of boots, of all the things twenty dollars could buy. He knew that the pawnkeeper had seen the instant's hesitation in his stride. He turned around and handed the pistol to the small man.

The pawnbroker handed him a double eagle.

"Got anything smaller?" They walked back into the shop.

The small man shrugged and gave him two five-dollar coins and ten silver dollars.

"Could you loan me a rag and some oil before my rifle goes to hell?" Dil asked.

The pawnbroker furnished him with a ramrod and watched interestedly as Dil strove to repair the ravages of a night's rain. "You need some ammunition for the rifle?"

Dil did and after some ritual haggling got twenty rounds a dime cheaper than he could have at the Mercantile. He struggled to control his raging hunger long enough to finish cleaning the rifle. Finally it was done.

"Where'd you get the pistol?" the pawnbroker asked.

"Off a man was shootin' at me," Dil said and exited while the pawnbroker was trying to decide whether to laugh or scream.

There had to be other eating places in a town the size of Winville but Dil had never noticed where they were. He strolled back toward the Jim Hill Hotel, marveling at how much better he felt already with almost nineteen dollars cash in his pocket.

When he had breakfasted he felt even more human. Still packing the 45-90, he stood in the street in front of the hotel, trying to decide what else to do. With the money he had now maybe he could buy a horse from Miz Haines. Then he realized that she would have none to spare. Nor could he get much of a horse for what would be left after he had gotten a new pair of boots. He went to the Mercantile.

Carrying considerably less weight in his pockets, he tried to decide whether walking the sixteen miles back up Bear Creek would be less painful in new boots than in this old. Neither way promised to be much fun.

Besides, now that he had eaten he was in no hurry. He had come to town to do something about Miss Hallie. There was nothing he could do back in Bear Creek. He tried to think. The car she had disappeared in was a Dodge. Would the courthouse know who owned a Dodge in this county? He should have gotten a license number, he guesed. But as long as he was here, what could he lose? He went to the courthouse, wincing at the feel of stiff new boots.

There was nobody in the lobby. He wondered if it was lunchtime already or if he had stumbled into the middle of one of those incomprehensible legal holidays that seemed invariably to fall on whatever day a rancher found a chance to get in to town.

Grumbling to himself, Dil went upstairs and abruptly realized that his feet were subconsciously leading him to the office where he had outbluffed a clerk who seemed to want him off his land almost as badly as everyone else seemed to.

Abruptly Dil's smoldering sense of outrage filled him. That little pen pusher knew something. He was already running scared. Dil considered the number of times he had been shot at. He remembered Al Haines. But most of all he remembered Miss Hallie. With the rifle in his hand he kicked open the door to the land office.

The green-eye-shaded clerk looked up and his face turned ashen. Dil vaulted over the railing, balancing his rifle with the muzzle pointed at the small man. He stepped around the desk and grasped the slack in the front of the clerk's shirt. The clerk looked like he was going to faint.

"Sheriff's dead," Dil said flatly. "I may do you a favor and kill you quick right now. On t'other hand, I might just put you in jail till the judge sees fit to hang you."

"H-hang me?" The clerk's astonishment overcame his fright.

"Sheriff told me a few things 'fore he died," Dil lied. "Now I want you t'tell me a few more."

The man's face was so ashen that Dil wondered if he might not die of fright. "Wh-what you want to know?" he managed. "I ain't done nothing."

"You know who done something," Dil snapped. "And

the law says if you knew and didn't tell nobody then you're gonna hang too."

"But I told the sheriff! He's the law, ain't he?"

Dil felt a sudden thrill of triumph. "Tell it to me, all slow and easy," he said. "And don't leave out any names."

"What you want to know?"

"Everything."

"Yeah, but—where do I start?"

Dil thought for a moment. "Who's Groby?" he asked.

"Game warden."

"Where'd he— Where's he live?"

But the little man who still dangled from the fistful of shirt Dil held caught his slip. His eyes widened and his face turned grayer. Dil fixed his gaze on the land office clerk. "Yup," he said. "You want to be next?"

Obviously the man in the green eye shade didn't.

"Where'd Groby live?"

"'Bout two miles out of town on the Bear Creek road."

Which, Dil calculated, would put the former game warden just about at the ford where Nellie's legs still poked obscenely skyward from her swollen carcass.

The clerk finally decided that he was not in imminent danger of dying. "Who you workin' for anyway?" he asked. "Them goddamn Indians?"

"Tell me all about them goddamn Indians," Dil said.

The clerk's green eye shade was knocked askew. He blinked up at Dil with surprise. "Put me down," he said. "I guess you got to start learnin' somewhere."

Dil took his hand off the other's shirt front. The clerk smoothed his ruffled feathers and sat down at his desk. "Just keep both hands in sight," Dil warned. "Now what is it I got to learn?"

"Some of the facts of life your folks must've never told you," the eye-shaded man said with the beginning of a sneer. "First off, there ain't nobody in this county gonna say 'no' if Mr. Richardson says 'yes.' "

"Who's Mr. Rich–" Abruptly Dil remembered the deputy's obsequious answers over the wind-up telephone when a mine manager had called to tell him, among other things, that the little scholarly-looking man in pince-nez and sheepskin vest was no longer sheriff. He thought for a moment. Mining companies and hydraulickers were birds of a feather. He wondered why it had taken him so long to see anything that obvious.

"You say the sheriff told you things," the clerk sneered. "Did you kill him before he got a chance t'tell you how he did everything a man in office could do for you Bear Creekers if that man expected to still be in office tomorrow?"

"I didn't kill him," Dil said.

The clerk was growing bolder all the time, anger and arrogance trying to make up for his funk of a moment ago. "I bet you tell that to all the men you kill."

"The sheriff died of a heart attack while up in Mr. Richardson's territory."

The clerk let out a long, sighing whistle and Dil could see him shrinking, deflating like a tire with a nail in it. After a moment he looked fixedly at Dil. "I've known him thirty years," he said. "*I'm* the one that has a bad heart." The clerk got slowly to his feet and went to the door. He opened it and peered up and down the hall. Turning back to Dil, he asked, "You see how it is?"

Dil shook his head.

"Then go away and think awhile. Grow up, boy! You come around here wavin' a rifle just as if I wasn't as good as dead already just for talkin' with you."

"You know anybody owns a Dodge touring car?"

The clerk shrugged off the question angrily. "Country's full of them." He was starting to say something else when he suddenly changed his mind. "Groby's got one," he said musingly. Then he was suddenly resolute. "Lunchtime'll be over soon. Get out of here before anybody sees us."

"I want some more information."

"Anything you want, but not here. Not now!"

"When?"

"Tonight, tomorrow. Any night. Just don't knock on the front door and don't knock at all if it looks like anybody else's there."

"Where?" Dil repeated.

The clerk scribbled on a piece of paper.

"I don't know any street names."

"Didn't figure you would. This's a map. If you're plannin' on gettin' killed, would you mind eating this before somebody finds it on you?" He pushed the map into Dil's hands and urged him toward the door.

"By the way," Dil asked from the doorway, "where can I find Joe Spokane?"

"Joe who? Oh! I don't know. Get out now. Try the Indian agency. Just go away, quick!" The little man was almost frantic again.

CHAPTER 14

Dil was striding out of town, still stiff and sore from last night's march through snow and rain, when he heard a flivver coming up the road behind him. His hands tightened around the 45-90 as he stepped to the side of the road. Groby was dead but he still didn't know what had happened to the other two dudes in four-cornered hats who had tried to ambush him by the pothole. He was wondering if he ought to step out and get the drop on them with the rifle long enough to go over the car for a bullet hole when he saw that it was starting to slow anyhow. When the flivver finally came abreast of him Dil saw that it held three dark, broad-faced men in pepper-and-salt suits. Joe Spokane was driving.

"Hello, Mr. Reeves," he called. "How goes the battle?"

The flivver's engine tried to stop, popped, and ran backward several turns before shuddering to death as dramatically as some road company Bernhardt. In the abrupt silence Dil told the three Indians how the battle was going. As he told the story he tried to guess from their noncommittal demeanor whether they had already heard the tale of Miss Hallie's abduction. When he ran down the three Indians still stared at him in silent contemplation. "Groby's dead?" Joe Spokane finally asked.

Dil nodded. "Leastways I think it was him. He was gone before I could show him to anybody else."

There was another silence. "So now you don't even have one horse. Where you heading?" Spokane asked. Dil realized dully that the young Indian was no longer using his elliptical style.

Dil sighed. "Out to see'f I can pick up any tracks after that bunch of taxpayers tromped up and down yesterday." Suddenly it began soaking into him that he was never going to see Miss Hallie alive again.

The man alone in the back seat of the flivver opened a door and moments later they were grinding in low gear through the ford where somebody—Groby, he guessed—had shot Nellie. He was about to yell at Joe Spokane when he saw that the Indian was already edging the flivver off the main road and down a path edged with drying, frostbitten weeds. A moment later they found Groby's cabin.

Actually, Dil realized, it was not a cabin. The game warden had lived in a small frame house built of sawn lumber, with casement windows that actually opened and closed, and had a tiny screened porch to one side. A frightened child's face peered through the screen. A moment later a middle-aged woman in poke bonnet came around from the side of the house where she had been poking a broomstick into a tub of clothes steaming over a small fire. Suddenly Dil snapped out of his apathy and his brain began working. "Mrs. Groby?" he asked, removing his hat.

The woman in the poke bonnet nodded.

"I'm Dil Reeves. The sheriff took me on as deputy just before he went north. We're tryin' to figure somethin' out. Man down the road a piece swears he didn't knock over no deer, says he was just lookin' when the game warden came along and did it. Course, it's all bunk but we gotta check. Could I see Mr. Groby's rifle?"

The poke-bonneted woman looked askance at the three pepper-and-salt-suited Indians. The three Indians tipped their hats politely. Mrs. Groby disappeared into the house and came out a moment later with a Krag-Jorgenson. She handed it to Dil.

Dil felt a moment of fierce triumph. His fleeting memory that Groby had not carried a rifle was paying off. He checked, saw that it was loaded, and walked to the horse trough. There was a hollow boom and splash of water. He fished the bullet from the green murk stirred up from the bottom of the trough and handed the weapon back to Mrs. Groby. "Thank you, ma'am," he said.

The woman in the poke bonnet gave him a shrewd look. "What makes you so sure it's all bunk?" she asked.

Dil didn't know what to say. The Indians tipped their hats again and backed the flivver around to head out of the yard. He supposed he should have broken the news to Mrs. Groby that she was a widow but he couldn't think of any easy way to explain who had made her a widow. "Back toward the ford," he yelled to Joe Spokane as they bounced out toward the Bear Creek road.

It was a messy job and several times Dil was ready to give up but finally, with the aid of a camp ax Joe produced from the hollow around the gas tank under the flivver's front seat, Dil managed to split open Nellie's forehead and plow through until he found a lump of lead. Squatting in the ford, he washed himself, scrubbing his hands and forearms repeatedly with sand until he was free of the smell. The lump of lead was so deformed that he couldn't tell for sure. Sighing, he bounced the two slugs in his hand, one perfect, the other mashed out of shape. Then abruptly he had another inspiration. "Could we go back into Winville a little while?"

Joe Spokane nodded and cranked life into the flivver.

The small man at the sign of the three gilded balls remembered Dil. "Something else?" he asked.

Dil handed him the two lead slugs. "Are they out of the same gun?" he asked.

The small man with the curly black beard pursed his lips. "No way to prove it," he said. "This one's mashed up too bad to see the rifling, but . . ." He combed his beard with his fingers and hummed to himself. After a moment he put one slug on each pan of his gold scales. The scales balanced.

"Same weight bullet, probably same caliber," Dil growled. "Now I'm ninety per cent sure who shot my Nellie horse. Only question is, what good's it gonna do me?"

"Only one man around here I know ever buys Krag ammunition," the pawnbroker said. Suddenly his face changed as he stared at Dil. "You shot Groby!"

"And he shot my horse, shot at me a couple of times, and if anybody was to look careful around where Al Haines died, it might turn out Groby shot him too. But he's dead now," Dil sighed. "Who're the two dudes in four-cornered hats that were with him?"

"Why you want to know that?" the pawnbroker asked.

Dil rounded on him. "Because them drygulchin' SOBs had Miss Hallie last time I saw 'em. Because if I catch 'em it don't make no matter whether Al Haines' girl is dead or not, them two shypokes is gonna be!"

Joe Spokane began cutting Dil out, herding him out of the pawn shop while expertly soft-soaping the black-bearded broker, thanking him profusely with a hypnotic flow of verbiage that would have shamed an Arab. They were stalking across the street toward the sheriff's office when the pawnbroker came running after them. "I know them!" he said eagerly. "Mercantile was out of blasting powder so they came to me."

Dil dug in his heels and spun around.

"Geologists, they called themselves. I got their signatures on the register. Sprague. Sprague and Breedon!" he said triumphantly.

"What's so important?" Joe Spokane asked.

Dil told him about the four capped sticks of dynamite in the stove he had liberated from Jake Nelson's cabin. The Indian whistled. Five minutes later the young deputy who by now seemed thoroughly at home in the office had heard the whole story.

"What d'you expect me to do?" the deputy asked.

"I expect you to do somethin' about bringin' in a couple of kidnappers and murderers!" Dil growled.

The deputy shifted in his chair. "This's a pretty big county," he began. "One man can't cover every little thing– Hey there, you goddamn savage, what you doin' with that telephone?"

But Joe Spokane was already cranking furiously. The deputy considered Dil and the other two pepper-and-salt-suited Indians standing in solid phalanx between him and the telephone. As he listened to Joe Spokane's polished and elegant phrases soft-soaping Sarah and convincing her to charge long-distance calls to the Bureau of Indian Affairs the deputy's hostility abruptly diminished. By the time Spokane's unctuous voice was tripping easily over malfeasance, changes of venue and U.S. marshals the deputy was not hostile at all.

"I was sure you'd see the urgency of the situation once it was properly explained with due emphasis on the salient points," Joe Spokane said to the deputy. He thanked Sarah and hung up. Turning back to the deputy, he added, "I'm sure you'll keep Mr. Richardson apprised of recent developments. Lately his group seems to be at loggerheads with the BIA—excuse me. We get into that habit in Washington. Bureau of Indian Affairs, I meant to say."

While the deputy was goggling and trying to think of some face-saving crusher the dapper Indian continued, "My colleagues and Mr. Reeves will be on our way now.

I trust you'll join us with a posse once you've aroused the citizenry of this good town."

"Where you goin'?"

"Why, out to kill or capture Mr. Groby's evil cohorts, of course, and to rescue the fair flower of Bear Creek. Oh yes, should you contact Mr. Richardson, it might be well to warn him that my people would not take it amiss if he were to furnish a small peace-keeping force. As you know, there are other, less-moderating influences in the tribe who feel strongly about any armed white man trespassing on reservation soil. And since my more impetuous tribesmen are all armed with modern hunting rifles we must hope cooler heads will prevail and that a buffer zone can be established to prevent unnecessary unpleasantness."

The deputy's mouth was still open when they closed the door and cranked some life into the flivver. Dil was having some trouble keeping his own closed. "What'd that all mean?" he asked.

Joe Spokane sighed. "Unfortunately, it's as empty as it sounds. I'd give our open-mouthed friend in there about half an hour before he recovers and starts checking and finds out the BIA office is closed this time of year." He gave a bitter smile. "Even when it's open, nothing ever happens there except talk and fine print. Where do you think I learned this kind of randygazoo?"

Dil looked bleakly at the Indian. "So what am I gonna do?" he asked.

Spokane shrugged. "No good fairies, no U. S. Cavalry, no noble redman gonna get you out of the hole. Like everyone else in this vale of tears, I suspect you're going to have to kill your own snakes if you have a fondness for going barefoot."

"But why'd you peddle the deputy all that bull about wantin' Richardson to send an army down here to the reservation?"

"Because I can usually count on any white man to do exactly what I ask him not to. This way your aroused citizenry of Bear Creek will stick to their part of it, below the gorge and my hotheaded militants: two eighty-year-olds with one broken shotgun between them will remain sun-warmed and happy on the reservation."

"How can you be sure? Won't somebody sneak across and start even more trouble?"

"You should have looked better at that contour map," Spokane said. "Unless you climb up through that Bear Creek gorge it's fifty miles around over the kind of roads the Great White Father sees fit to build on reservations. I doubt if any of your Bear Creekers can tear themselves away long enough to go around. And it'd take a better mountain climber than I to go through."

"Oh." Dil was deflated and defeated. "Ain't even got a horse anymore," he muttered.

Spokane gave a shrug of commiseration. "We'll give you a ride out home. Seems the least we can do. I'm sorry about your girl."

The sixteen miles of bumpy ruts passed by in grim silence as Dil surveyed the wreckage of his hopes. He had lost both horses, his first friend, and his friend's daughter. Now when it was too late he realized that the scholarly little man in the pince-nez had been doing his best to help him, doing everything he could do if he expected to hold his job. Slowly the realization grew on him that he was fighting an octopus, lopping off tentacles madly without once reaching the nerve center that kept sending out killer after killer to do him dirty.

"Richardson!" he snarled.

Joe Spokane heard him over the moan of the slipping low band. "Correct," he said. "Or at least it's a step in the right direction. You must remember that even Mr. Richardson is only an employee, paid by someone higher up to make a profit from mining. One of the easiest ways to make a profit is to own the local courthouse."

"Why?"

Spokane gave him an odd look. "Why'd the sheriff go up to the north county in the first place?"

"I don't know—oh, yeah! To break a strike."

"Exactly. To defeat several hundred men's effort to get a living wage for a day's dirty and dangerous work."

Dil had never thought of it that way before. "You a wobblie?" he asked.

Spokane shrugged and wrenched the wheel across a set of ruts. "I'd be much worse if I thought it might keep my people from being winterkilled. Have you never wondered why you manage to stay poor no matter how hard you work?"

Dil had but he felt that he was skirting a dangerous heresy. They were within a mile of his cabin and if the Indians were to make it back to town before dark there could be no loitering. He sat glumly in the rear seat of the bouncing flivver, wondering what he was going to do. He was less than a hundred yards from home when he saw old Bill grazing on the soggy, winterkilled grass. The horse looked accusingly at him and whinnied.

To his embarrassment, Dil found his eyes full of tears. He pounded Joe Spokane on the back and bounded from the flivver. It was moving faster than he had thought and he tumbled several times before gaining his feet. Bill stared with as much curiosity as an old horse could muster. Dil thanked the Indians, who struggled to conceal their amusement. "If you get time, would you stop on the way back and tell Miz Haines I'm home and everything."

Spokane nodded gravely. "What shall I tell her you're doing?"

"Guess I'll go look for Miss Hallie," Dil said. "If I can just think of where to start."

The Indians made their farewells and he stood beside old Bill on the pathway to his lean-to. Slowly he led the horse back down the path. The lean-to was deserted and seemed untouched since the last time he had been here. It wasn't until he was inside that he saw the body stretched out before Jake Nelson's cold stove.

CHAPTER 15

Ants had somehow resurrected from their incipient hibernation and were crawling over the dead man. A rat scurried away as Dil moved closer. So this, he mused, was where Groby had ended up. He wondered where they had stashed the body while all the Bear Creekers were up here blundering around. After standing indecisive for a minute he dragged the body outside and fetched a bucket of water from the creek. He washed his hands and began making biscuits.

It was nearing sundown by the time he had satisfied his hunger. What to do now? He had old Bill again. He wondered. Now that he had a body, he had some real proof that Miss Hallie had been kidnapped. He wondered if Miz Haines had ever been convinced in her own mind that Dil had not had some hand in her daughter's disappearance. Maybe now with some proof he could go back to town and raise enough stink for a thorough manhunt. Any way he looked at it, he wasn't doing anything to get Miss Hallie back by sticking around here. Sighing at the thought of another night journey in to town, he began rigging a diamond hitch to get the dead game warden atop old Bill. The sun was still up as he started the sixteen miles back to town, sitting uncomfortably forward on Bill's shoulders, feeling the stiff body bump him behind at every step of the old horse's trot.

After a couple of miles of it he got off and walked, leading Bill. Shadows began lengthening as he passed the pothole where loons shrieked and where a trio of varmints in a flivver had set up an ambush for him the other night. This evening he had the road to himself. He wondered what had been the point in planting the body in his lean-to. Surely there had to be a reason. He wondered if Groby's two friends would have assumed that he'd kept quiet about shooting the big man. Could they expect to turn it into a murder charge against Dil? With the kind of law Richardson imposed in this county Dil guessed that anything was possible.

Perhaps he ought just to dump the body somewhere in the woods far enough away from the road for the coyotes to finish him off before spring. . . . But after he considered this for a while Dil decided that this body was still his only real proof that somebody else had taken Miss Hallie. He had to bring it in unless he was willing to write her off.

He remembered her shy smile, the way she had tagged along with him, not wanting to ride alone down the opposite side of the canyon the day they were hunting livestock. Probably dead by now. He guessed that he owed her memory something. Her pa's too. He blinked angry tears from his eyes and struggled down the road in gathering darkness. Suddenly he was opposite the Haines' pathway. He guessed no matter how late it was he ought to stop a minute and let Miz Haines know how things were.

He remembered that the dog and her pups were dead. Remembering too that Miz Haines was alone in the house and possibly prepared for another kind of a visit, he began shouting and hallooing long before he was within gunshot.

Miz Haines had a lamp in the window by the time he came in sight of the house. He tied old Bill to the pump handle and walked toward the house. Miz Haines stepped behind him, appearing out of the darkness with a cocked pistol. "Just put down your rifle and march on into the house," she said.

Feeling extremely prickly around the back of his neck, Dil did so. In the kitchen, where she could see his face, Miz Haines finally relaxed and stopped pointing the gun at him. "So it's you," she said defeatedly.

Dil tried to breathe normally. "You been havin' more trouble?"

"Ain't I got enough?"

Dil guessed that she did. Miz Haines had been comfortably rounded the first day he'd seen her. Now she was gaunt, with angular boniness showing through in unexpected places.

"Who you got on the horse?" she asked. "I can see it ain't Hallie."

"Groby," Dil said. "He was one of the varmints that got her."

Miz Haines caught up her Colt again. She picked up the kerosene lamp in her left hand and went toward the door. Dil opened it for her and they went out to the pump, where old Bill stood with equine patience. Miz Haines struggled ineffectually at the tarp, unwilling to let go of lamp or pistol. Dil worked at the knots and got a corner open. Miz Haines spent a long time looking at the dead man's face. Finally she turned back to Dil. "I don't know who you got there," she said, "but that isn't Groby."

"But I—" Dil protested. "That's the man I creased with a bullet one day he was huntin' me. He's the same one was leadin' Miss Hallie's horse when they had her blindfolded."

"I don't care if he cut St. Peter's throat with a billiard ball," Miz Haines said grimly. "Groby lives a spell down the creek and I know him well enough."

Abruptly Dil remembered the equanimity with which Mrs. Groby had produced her husband's rifle. She had not acted like a grieving widow. He had thought that she didn't know yet. Instead, she must have seen her husband recently enough not to have been worried about him. Which meant . . .

He looked at Miz Haines. "Is there anybody along this creek you think might be dirty enough to help hide Miss Hallie?"

Miz Haines thought for a moment. "Can't think of anyone," she said, "except maybe old Groby."

Which was exactly what Dil had been thinking. "He shot my Nellie horse a few days ago. I got proof of that now."

Miz Haines' hand holding the lamp shook. Dil caught it before the chimney could fall off. They went back into the kitchen. "I'll fix a lunch," she said in that same flat tone, "if you'll go harness up the buckboard."

Dil nodded and went out to the barn.

They trotted through the night, leading old Bill behind the buckboard. Miz Haines had her husband's Colts belted around her waist. Dil still carried his 45-90. He considered borrowing one of her pistols but he knew that he wouldn't be able to hit anything with it. He checked the action on his rifle.

"You think maybe we ought to go on in to town first and do it legal-like?" Dil asked.

"Ain't you got your fill yet of the way they do things in town?"

Dil guessed that he had. He fingered through his pockets nervously, was overcome with a sudden doubt, and unloaded his 45-90 to check a round of the new ammunition. It fit. He had enough for a prolonged battle. He hoped to God it wouldn't come to that.

Finally they were near the turn-off to Groby's place. "You ever been there?" Dil asked. Miz Haines hadn't. He described the layout to her as well as he could remember.

Miz Haines nodded grimly. "We'll tie the buckboard

here," she explained. Moments later they were walking along the brush-lined path into Groby's farmyard. Dil waited for the dogs to start up. For some reason they didn't. The house loomed and to Dil's surprise there was a light showing through one curtained window.

They stopped and surveyed each other in the darkness. "You want to flip for it?" Miz Haines asked.

"No. I was there this afternoon. I go knockin' on the door and—" He left it dangling.

"I'll go 'round back," Miz Haines whispered. "When you figure I've had time you go make some deputy-sheriff noises at the front door."

Dil nodded and waited while Miz Haines slipped off into the darkness with a stealth surprising in so large a woman. He expected the dogs to start barking at any moment. He decided that they must be off on a nightly coon hunt or some such canine pastime or they would have been busy by now. He began moving quietly toward the only window that showed a light. Inside, two men were arguing angrily. He strained to hear what they were saying. The lamplight filtered through a white gauze curtain was so diffuse that he could not get a clear look at their faces. One man wore a hat. It was, he suddenly realized, an engineer's hat with four dents in the crown and a flat brim.

Suddenly one voice rang loud and clear. ". . . stupid lot of bunglers! I told you it was to be done within strictly legal methods and now you've laid us wide open on murder and kidnapping and heaven only knows what else! Do you realize what it's going to cost the company to straighten out a mess like this?"

The other man made vague mollifying noises. Dil decided that he had heard enough. He went around to the door and pounded. "Mr. Groby!" he called in a shrill voice, "Mr. Groby, somethin' awful's happened!"

There was a commotion of scraping chairs inside the house, then the door burst open. "What the hell's going on?"

The man inside the house was not a complete fool. He had left the lamp behind in the other room. When the door opened it was even darker than outside where Dil stood. Dil squinted into the blackened rectangle of the doorway. "Mr. Groby?" he asked again. He seemed to be having trouble with his voice.

"You!"

Abruptly Dil caught sight of the man in the doorway. Groby had been in a lamplit room and could see outside no better than Dil could see in. But he was squatting, hands going to his belt as he settled into a hipshooter's crouch. Dil realized that, as usual, he had been caught unprepared. It wasn't supposed to work this way at all. The game warden was supposed to collapse in terror at the sight of a rifle trained on him, supposed to beg for mercy and bleat confessions and do all the craven things done by those not girded with righteousness. Instead, the SOB was going to kill him before he could even aim the 45-90!

Dil struggled to raise the octagonal barrel of the heavy rifle. It was swinging as slowly as a broom handle in a molasses barrel. His thumb frantically slid over hammer and safety. It was cocked. He willed himself to pull the trigger quickly, now! Get it done before the shadowy figure before him could finish settling into that gunfighter's stance. This was one of the three men in the flivver with funny hats and surveyor's transit whom he had pulled out of the mud up by the pothole. Probably, he guessed, it was the one who had called him a rube. And it would have been so easy to be on friendly terms with them. . . .

Dil wondered where he had gone wrong. Somehow, from the start, he had gotten off on the wrong foot with this trio of city dudes. He wondered why it had to be this way; but mostly he wondered if his paralyzed trigger finger would ever move.

There was a sudden lightninglike illumination as a foot-long flame erupted from the muzzle of his rifle. At the same time twin roman candles spurted from Groby's hands. In the brief flicker of daylight Dil saw the hatless man's face clearly for the first time. It was the one who called him a rube.

Dil jacked another shell into the rifle, wondering if he had been hit, wondering if he had hit the other man. Groby was spinning, shifting to make himself a smaller target. Then slowly Dil realized that he was spinning from the push of a piece of lead nearly a half inch wide. He jacked at his rifle again, ejecting a perfectly good cartridge, and realized that he was coming down with a classic case of buck fever.

Dil bounded over the collapsing Groby, toward the light-filled doorway behind him. When he got there the room where Groby had been conferring with the other man was empty. He picked up the lamp in his left hand and moved cautiously toward the next room. Mrs. Groby sat up in the bed, her face drawn with terror. A child huddled next to her.

Dil was suddenly overcome with doubts again. What was he doing with a rifle in some strange woman's bedroom? He didn't belong here. This was the kind of thing the bad guys did.

He gestured toward the front door with the muzzle of the 45-90. "Take your young'un and git!" he snapped. "They's probably gonna be some more shootin'!"

Clad in a flannel nightgown and lace cap, Mrs. Groby stopped long enough to grab a patchwork quilt off the bed before she scurried past him over Groby's body and out the front door. A moment later there was a shot and a scream. Dil felt a sudden sickness descend upon him.

He stood wobbling for a moment in the bedroom, forcing himself to breathe deeply. The other city dude was alive and kicking somewhere. Dil realized how perfect a target he was with an oil lamp in his hands. He put it down and checked his rifle again. Creeping through the darkness toward the back of the house, he tried to consider how many possibilities were left before him.

Standing just inside the open back door and to one side, he called, "Miz Haines, you all right?"

There was no answer. Dil went back to the bedroom and blew out the lamp. He felt his way through the house, listening to the night sounds, ears straining for the slightest clue. By the time he had fumbled his way back over Groby's stiffening body to the front door his eyes were reaccustoming to darkness.

"Miz Haines," he called, "you out there anywhere?"

Still no answer. He wondered if the other city dude had shot Mrs. Groby. Then he wondered if Miz Haines had shot her. Or . . . could Mrs. Groby have managed to conceal a handgun under that quilt? Suddenly he knew with a sickly certainty what had happened. He knelt to fumble over Groby's inert body. Both of the pistols that had aimed a single shot apiece at him in the darkness were gone now. Somewhere out there in the brush Mrs. Groby was waiting. She must have gotten Miz Haines with that first shot.

CHAPTER 16

The silence grew cold and tense. Dil dithered alone in the darkened house. Mrs. Groby had probably stashed her infant somewhere off in the brush. Now she was waiting, waiting out in the darkness where she knew every step, every hole, hollow, and stumble, waiting for Dil to show his head. He felt a sudden sympathy for the caged bird he had once won in a turkey shoot.

It just wasn't fair. He was doing his goddamnedest to act like a man. And here he was caught up in a shootin' match between two women! Even if he ever got out of here alive, Dil suspected that he would never be able to face the sneers and snickers in Winville once his ridiculous plight became known. And where was Miss Hallie? Now it looked like he was going to die without ever finding out.

Somewhere miles away he heard the faint racket of an automobile. A dog barked. But closeby there were no sounds. Not the slightest hint of breathing, snap of twig, or rustle of grass that could tell him where she was.

And this time, Dil knew, there wouldn't even be an inquiry into his death. Mrs. Groby could add to the story he had already told on himself. Earlier he had claimed to have killed Groby. This time he had made good his claim, shot the game warden inside the doorway to his own house. Nobody could have any complaints if Mrs. Groby returned the compliment.

He had to get out of here. Time was not on his side. If

Mrs. Groby decided that he was going to sit it out she could curl up in the comforter with her child and wait for sunup. Each hour he waited made things that much worse. Or . . . she might have hotfooted it to town. It was only two or three miles from here to Winville. How long before she was back with that deputy sheriff the mine owners had in their hip pocket?

He felt his way about the house, feeling blindly, absently seeking inspiration. His fist closed over a heavy crockery cup. It seemed a shame to destroy somebody's valuable household furnishings, but . . . Standing well back behind the dead Groby, he overhanded the cup out the open front door. It crashed loudly somewhere out in the yard.

When nothing happened he reflected ruefully on his earlier luck tossing pine cones. He felt his way back into the kitchen and fumbled about blindly, praying that he wasn't making so much noise that Mrs. Groby could tell which part of the house he was in. Finally his groping hands found the broom in the hollow between the range and the woodbox. He took off his hat and arranged it with some care on the business end of the broom. Another long, stumbling fumble through the darkness. His feet tangled with Groby's stiffening form. Then he was cautiously sticking the hat-clad broom out the door, turning it slowly like somebody peering into the night.

Mrs. Groby wasn't buying it. He pulled the broom back in disgustedly and put his hat back on. Then he changed his mind and went to the back door to try the same trick. Still nothing happened. Abruptly he realized that he might be writing the scenario all wrong. He had forgotten about the third city dude in four-cornered hat. He had been in the house when Dil shot Groby. He had made a beeline out the back door and somehow gotten by Miz Haines. Or had he somehow managed silently to put her out of action?

He remembered the shot and scream as Mrs. Groby and her child had scurried out the front door. He gave it long and serious thought and came to the conclusion that he hadn't the slightest idea what was going on out there in the darkness. He stuck the behatted broom out the back door and tried to make it move like a cautious man's head. If anyone was watching he didn't fall for it.

Dil went around the house, opening casement windows, trying the broom-and-hat trick on every side. He opened the door out onto the screen porch. There was a bed out there that had been slept in recently but it was empty.

Utterly defeated, he stood in the middle of the screened porch, controlling his ragged breathing, fighting off the fit of trembling that threatened to overcome him now that he had had time to simmer down from the fine, high emotion of killing Groby. Somewhere in the barnyard he thought he heard something. No matter how he listened the sound did not repeat itself.

Faintly on the edge of his attention an automobile putted through the night, seeming no closer than the last time he had heard it. Even farther away came the distant shriek of a screech owl. Then close, not over half a mile off, he heard the coughing grunt of a hunting cougar. But in the barnyard, around the house, there was not the faintest whisper of wind to help hide the fact that there was no sound at all. Dil carefully released a long-held breath, struggling to preserve the silence.

It was a Mexican standoff. But . . . He struggled to fit the pieces together. There was the other city dude who had been chewing out Groby. Suddenly he realized who this just might be. "*Do you realize what it's going to cost the company to straighten out a mess like this?*" There was only one person in the county who would talk like that.

He wondered if the mining company manager had brought the dead sheriff's body back to Winville or if he was here for other business. Obviously Mr. Richardson had been poking around Bear Creek for some time. Just as obviously, he might remember Dil's face from the day he had pulled the three dudes out of the mud. But . . . Dil thought for a moment. Unless he had known that somebody was listening, which seemed unlikely, then he could not have been along the night that several shadows in a flivver had laid an ambush along the flat by the pothole and received a potshot at their darkened flivver instead. Dil wondered exactly where Richardson stood in this mess. Was he hanging around outside, waiting for a shot at Dil? Or had he hightailed it to town immediately?

Managers, if Dil understood the word right, managed. That meant they inveigled somebody else into doing the actual dirty work. Richardson would be long gone. And Mrs. Groby? He wondered if that single sharp scream had come from her or from Miz Haines.

How much time had passed since then? It seemed hours but Dil guessed that it couldn't have been more than four or five minutes. He put his hat on the broom again for another try. A minute later he had made another circuit of the house, peeking with hat and broom out of every door and window. If anyone waited out there they were waiting for a better shot, for him to step clear of the house. If something didn't happen soon Dil was afraid that he might have to risk it.

Irrationally his mind fastened on Hallie. If she was still alive she was probably a double orphan by now. If she was alive and if he survived this night—if he ever saw her alive again—what was he going to do about her? He remembered her reluctance to go alone down the opposite side of the valley the day they had been hunting run-off stock. Was he indulging in wishful thinking or had she really wanted to be close to him?

He wondered how Mrs. Groby had managed, short of strangling it, to make her infant keep from making noise. Any kid he had ever known would be shrieking its head off after all these nocturnal shenanigans. He hoped that the child was safe somewhere off in the brush. He wasn't particularly fond of the prospect of shooting Mrs. Groby, even if she was gunning for him with both hands. But if she had a child in her arms Dil knew that he was as good as dead.

How long had he been in this house? A half hour or a half minute? He had lost all track of time. Remembering the first time he had knocked over a deer, Dil knew that time could be deceptive. He tried to think. He had tried the hat-and-broom trick twice. He guessed that at least five or ten minutes had passed. Abruptly he remembered old Bill tied to the end of the buckboard out near the main road. He strained his ears but if the three horses were still there they were being as quiet as he was. The silence in the yard around the house was total, not a sigh, whisper, or muffled complaint of the child, who had to be fully awake after all the shooting and being dragged out into the middle of the chill night. He wondered if Mrs. Groby had lit out for town immediately. Maybe he was just standing here in the dark in the middle of her house waiting for that hip-pocket deputy to come out and kill him.

He had to get out of here, out into the darkness where he could skulk around on an equal basis with the rest of them. Once more he made a circuit of the house, fumbling and stumbling through the darkness, hunting for something—anything. In the bedroom, next to the door, he found a clothes tree which Groby apparently had used in lieu of a wardrobe. A hat and a coat of almost Prince Albert length hung from the wooden device.

Dil hefted it. Light enough. He removed Groby's hat and substituted his own. He silhouetted the assembly in the bedroom window and guessed that in the faint light from outside it just might resemble a man. A man wearing Dil's hat. He knelt and practiced carrying it while wriggling along on his knees. It was a forlorn hope but it might draw the first shot and give him something at which to aim. Stepping over Groby's stiffening body, he began a careful duck walk out the front door, holding before him the erect clothes horse with his hat and Groby's long coat.

Nothing happened. He crept through the yard, balancing the teetering clothes horse in front of him, squinting at the sky and praying that the sliver of moon would stay hidden behind snow clouds that moved swiftly from the northeast. It looked like the Indian summer was over as quickly as it had begun. By morning it would be snowing again. And Hallie, if she was still alive, was out there somewhere. Miz Haines . . . ?

There was a clump of brush past the place where Mrs. Groby had been poking a stick into a steaming tubful of clothes the last time he had visited this place. He began creeping toward it, praying that there would not be some sudden rift in the snow clouds to give him away. It was harder work than he had expected to carry the clothes horse upright in front of him, trying to make it move like a man and hanging on to his 45-90 at the same time. For an instant he questioned the wisdom of selling the pistol this morning, then knew that he could not have trusted himself to hit the broad side of a barn with it even if he hadn't been in dire danger of starving to death. At least he had eaten. It was comforting to know that he would die on a full stomach. He eased away from the house, toward the clump of brush, heading vaguely toward the horse trough where he had collected an unblemished bullet from Groby's Krag-Jorgenson this morning. And still nobody shot at him.

He began to feel distinctly foolish. They all must have lit running, not caring to contest with this wild-eyed man with the rifle who had appeared suddenly in the middle of the night and gunned down the owner of this house. Dil wondered if someday some prosecutor might not be putting it just like that to twelve carefully selected citizens from the other end of the county—miners who neither knew nor cared what was going on in Bear Creek.

A week ago he had been a law-abiding young man minding his own business, trying to get set for the winter. Now . . . If Miz Haines had disappeared along with her daughter—abruptly he realized that it would not require an especially clever prosecutor to convict him not only of Groby's murder, but of all three members of the Haines family. And the hell of it was, in a way he felt responsible for all three of them.

Dil knew that he shouldn't have let Al Haines ride in to town with him. He had been shot at already. He should have known that it would happen again. He had let Miss Hallie ride off down the opposite side of the canyon when she had most obviously not wanted to. And now he had, against his better judgment, let Miz Haines come along with him on this abortive business—just as if a woman had any place in a gunfight!

He was so sickened with disgust at his stupidity that he almost stood up and let the clothes tree fall. It would serve him right to die now. Miss Hallie was dead, along with both of her parents. Even if she was alive, how could she ever forgive him for the careless way he had let Mr. Richardson's hired guns finish off both her parents?

Slowly he waddled toward the deeper darkness, carrying the clothes tree in front of him, struggling to hang on to his 45-90. He had nearly reached the deeper darkness of the buckbrush. This was a foolish business, he knew. They all had lit running long ago. He was all alone here in Groby's yard. Why was he making a fool of himself creeping about with a decoy? He was about to let go of it and stand up when he felt an arm snake around his neck from behind. The arm began choking him.

CHAPTER 17

The clothes tree fell with a clatter. He felt his rifle slip from his hands, then realized dimly that somebody else was catching it before the cocked piece could hit the ground and rouse the countryside. The arm across his throat was threatening to crush his Adam's apple. Dil wanted to struggle but he was too weak, too sick with disgust, to care any longer what happened to him. Any way he looked at it, he was licked. A sensible man had to know when to give up.

"Quiet!" a voice whispered in his ear. "Don't make any noise."

"Who?" he managed in a croaking whisper.

"Joe Spokane."

Immediately Dil's depression was over. He relaxed and a moment later the pressure on his windpipe lessened. He allowed himself to be led-dragged into the deeper shadow of the buckbrush. "How many people here and what's the situation?" Spokane whispered.

Dil captured the Indian's ear and spent nearly a minute explaining what was going on, keeping his whisper as inaudible as the other's. He remembered the distant sound of an automobile and wondered how far away the Indians had left it. Then abruptly he remembered Miz Haines' buckboard. He asked about it.

"Not there," Spokane replied. "We combed the place pretty thoroughly."

"Now what?" Dil asked himself. He had listened to the

best of his ability and had not heard the three horses trot away. But . . . abruptly he realized that the trees and brush must have muffled sounds much better than he had thought, for he had heard only an automobile miles away on the extreme edge of audibility and still Joe Spokane was here. "Is there anybody hiding around here in the brush?" Dil asked.

Joe Spokane didn't think there was. Gradually they stopped whispering and slipped into normal speaking voices. "You ain't seen Miz Haines or Groby's wife?" Dil asked. When Joe said that he hadn't Dil sighed. "I'd give six bits to know what's goin' on," he groused.

"You say you shot someone?"

"It was him or me," Dil said defensively.

"Let's take a look."

Gingerly Dil made his way back across the yard he had crossed so painstakingly with a clothes horse. Nothing happened. He heard Joe close the door behind him. He fumbled his way back to where he had left the lamp and after another interminable stumble found a seven-day stink in a baking powder can nailed to the wall between woodbox and range.

Joe Spokane squatted to study the body in the lamplight behind the closed door. "You always shoot that way?" he asked.

Dil studied the body. The bridge of Groby's nose had been driven inward, giving him a vaguely Oriental look. "Not always," Dil admitted. "Leastways, not in the dark."

Spokane straightened and faced Dil. "With the decedent's pistols gone and he dead on his own doorstep, the legal consequences could be awkward," he said.

"I've had a little while to think about that too," Dil agreed. "And if Richardson gets to that deputy first he may be able to pin Miss Hallie, Miz Haines—hell, I might end up gettin' hung for everybody!"

"Richardson? The mine superintendent?"

"Well," Dil said, "the way he was snarlin' and snappin' about gettin' the company in trouble and the way Groby was just sittin' there saying yes, sir, yes, sir, I figured it just about had to be Mr. Richardson from up in north county."

Joe Spokane slapped his forehead. "You're right!" he said exultantly. "It has to be!"

"By the way, where are your friends?"

"On the way to the reservation, I hope; spreading the word not to let anybody provoke us into a shootout we'll most assuredly lose."

There seemed to be nothing to say. Dil searched the house again, this time with the lamp in his left hand and the rifle in his right. There was nothing remarkable, though he wished he could afford Groby's taste in brass beds and morris chairs. He peeked out onto the screened porch doubtfully, then, reassured that Joe Spokane had been over the grounds already, he stepped out to see what the lean-to contained.

Apart from a slept-in bed it contained nothing much. Odds and ends of harness and saddle gear hung from pegs. In the corner was an empty nose bag and a pair of worn boots. Spokane glanced at the screened sides of the porch and stepped out gingerly into the lit area where Dil held the lamp. He kicked at a short piece of rope next to the bed. "Odd sort of thing to keep in a bedroom," he remarked.

Dil glanced at the short pieces of rope with fresh-cut ends. He looked once more at the nose bag and remembered his last glimpse of Hallie, hands tied, bag over her head, as one man led her horse and another followed.

"So this is where they kept her," he muttered.

Joe Spokane bent over the bed and threw back the blankets. He buried his nose in the covers for an instant, then sniffed the pillow. He nodded at Dil.

"You can smell her, just like a houn'dog?" Dil marveled.

The Indian gave a wintery smile. "If you'd grown up in a large family and a small house I'm sure you'd have no trouble sniffing out the differences between a man and a woman—or a young woman from an old one. I'll not swear this bed has been occupied by your lady love. But it's been occupied by a young female who normally takes better care of herself."

"How long ago was she here?"

Spokane shrugged. "Half an hour."

Irrelevantly Dil noticed that the Indian had foregone his pepper-and-salt suit for the first time and was clad in Levis and a brilliant flannel shirt. But what, he asked himself, had gone wrong? Miz Haines had been set with twin Colts out there somewhere in the brush. He sighed. There was only one way Richardson could have gotten Miss Hallie out the back door while he was arranging details with Groby. If Miss Hallie had been taken away from here, it had been over Miz Haines' dead body.

He stared bleakly at the Indian. "No more fancy words?"

Spokane shrugged. "There comes a time when only actions will suffice. Where would an influential man unused to violence take a captive girl?"

Dil didn't have the slightest idea. "Somewhere in town?" he asked.

Spokane glanced nervously at the screen. They were perfect targets out here on the porch. Dil took the lamp back into the kitchen and they sat facing each other across the table. "I think we can rule out anywhere in town," Spokane said. "Our man Richardson is as much of a victim as you are."

Dil just looked at him.

"He didn't intend things to go this far. If you're reporting accurately, he wanted to put a little pressure on the

Bear Creekers and encourage them to sell out or forfeit. Now suddenly he's up to his neck in murders and kidnappings. He won't know where to turn but he knows this kind of thing can't be hushed up indefinitely. Subordinates who'll wink at coercion or collusion just may balk at the thought of murder—especially if it involves a nubile white girl."

Dil didn't understand half the words. He wanted to ask what "nubile" meant but Spokane was maundering on, seemingly more to himself than to Dil.

"A man used to delegating authority suddenly finds himself faced with the dirty job he used to hand somebody else. Will he try to delegate authority again? Or will he cut his losses and get out? You heard only one shot?"

Dil nodded.

"And we find no body. Which means two out of three women exited these premises alive. Which two?"

Dil didn't know. He studied Joe Spokane's dark, broad face, trying to figure what the Indian was getting at. He wondered if Mr. Richardson had shot Hallie. It would make sense from the mine manager's viewpoint. He would see her as the only one who could tie him in with the kidnapping. Then Dil saw the hole in that argument. Mrs. Groby had just lost a husband. Where would her loyalty lie?

"Unless Mr. Richardson is unusually perceptive," Spokane continued, "he may still be involved in the decision process, searching for some bloodless solution to his dilemma. Now where would a man not well acquainted with Bear Creek decide to hole up with several recalcitrant female captives?"

Afterward Dil was to wonder what process of intuition and elimination brought it out of him with such rapidity. At the moment he listened in amazement as his own voice blurted, "Jake Nelson's cabin!"

Joe Spokane considered Dil's words. "Apart from your place that would be the only other unoccupied house on Bear Creek. It's within reasonable distance, and there's reason to presume Mr. Richardson and his cohorts know the premises if they spent any time poisoning Nelson's attitude toward you. Next question: How well do *you* know the premises?"

Dil wasn't sure. He remembered the general layout of the cabin and pole corral from the day he had looted the stove from the man he had been forced to kill, whose death had been the first in this seemingly endless string of killings. "I guess I could find my way. You think we ought to get some help?"

"Mr. Richardson is a sorely pressed man. Soon he may reach the only viable decision from his standpoint. Besides, upon whom would you call for re-enforcements?"

Dil remembered the trigger-happy Bear Creekers' fizzle the day when Miss Hallie had been taken. He guessed that the Indian was right. Abruptly he understood some of Spokane's high-flown verbiage and knew that "viable decision" meant that Mr. Richardson was going to have to kill Miss Hallie if he wanted to save his own hide. "Let's go!"

Spokane cupped his hand next to the lamp chimney and blew. They left the darkened house and began walking down the path toward the Bear Creek road. The buckboard and old Bill were gone. So was the body he had loaded atop the old horse. Silently they walked up the darkened road toward Dil's place, toward Jake Nelson's empty and stoveless cabin.

Overhead a sliver of moon peeped intermittently from snow clouds. Abruptly Dil realized what was wrong with their hastily organized raid. "You ain't got no gun!" he said accusingly.

"How observant of you," the Indian said dryly.

"But–"

Spokane shrugged. "Though your peerless protector of public probity sees fit to call me a savage, I must insist that I have never been a man of violence." He was silent for a moment. "Not to say that I have not on occasion contributed my share of meat to the general fund. But it takes an extremely dull child not to realize there are more of you than of us, and that when it comes to the cruel and unusual, your forefathers knew themselves well enough to write certain provisos into their Constitution. I have dedicated my life to trying to make that Constitution apply to Indians as well as whites. By the way, did you know scalping was invented by a British officer to keep score on the body count in one of your interminable wars?"

Dil hadn't known. All he knew was that they were alone on a dark road, heading toward trouble, and all that they had between them was his father's venerable 45-90. He counted the shells in his pocket. Suddenly he wished that he'd remembered to pick up the one he had jacked out of the rifle when he'd gotten buck fever shooting Groby. He wondered if he would ever get used to shooting men. So far he'd killed three. A week ago he wouldn't have believed he could point a gun at a man and pull the trigger. But then, a week ago he couldn't have imagined that anyone in the world would want to kill him.

There was a shriek, prolonged and agonized, with a soul-chilling quality that nearly made him drop his rifle before he realized that it was just another loon. They walked a mile in silence while Dil struggled to quiet his shattered nerves and still the trembling in his hands. If he had to shoot anybody right now he knew that he couldn't hit the nonlethal end of a bull with a snow shovel.

Occasionally Joe Spokane put a hand on his arm and they stood for a moment, listening. Apart from the distant drumming of a partridge one time the night was silent. They were nearly at the turn-off to Jake Nelson's cabin when the Indian stopped again. Dil heard the faint sound again. Abruptly he wondered what a partridge was doing out courting at this time of night and at this time of year!

His companion seemed unperturbed. Dil wondered if the Indian's instincts had been dulled by all the years it must have taken him to learn his hyperbolic style of talk. Then he remembered how neatly an arm had come out of the darkness to terminate his skulk behind the clothes horse.

He wished that there were somebody he could trust to help them. But, remembering the way the Bear Creekers had shot up the underbrush the day Miss Hallie had been taken . . . It was going to be hard enough going it alone but this way he had the only firearm. If he heard another shot he would know that it was meant for him. But that wouldn't make it any easier. There were at least two women running around these woods somewhere. Maybe three. If they were in Jake Nelson's cabin and somebody started shooting at him from that cabin, what was he going to do?

Dil didn't know. He took a deep breath and tried to move down the path as soundlessly as his partner.

CHAPTER 18

Joe Spokane touched his arm and they stood silent for a moment. A sliver of moon peeped momentarily from the scudding snow clouds and he saw the vague, looming lump of darkness beside the pole corral. Somewhere on the edge of audibility a partridge drummed an out-of-season rhythm. He remembered how he and Miz Haines had split up the last time he had assaulted a cabin—and what a disaster that had turned into.

"What do we do now?" he whispered.

The Indian was apparently in some doubt too. "Wait awhile," he whispered back.

Dil stood fidgeting in the darkness, gripping the 45-90. He wanted to check the action but the sound would carry for half a mile in this tomblike stillness beneath the snow clouds. Anyway, it was only a kind of nervous tic. He knew that the rifle was loaded. All he had to do was cock it and squeeze the trigger and a piece of lead nearly half an inch thick would leave the muzzle, moving so slowly that one could almost see it, yet moving fast enough to knock down man or beast and tear a tremendous lethal hole in whatever it hit—if he could hit anything in this darkness.

He squinted at the dark outline of the cabin and the pole corral, trying to remember what it had been like the day he came for the stove. There was not the slightest hint of light or sound from the cabin. He began to wonder if there was anyone there at all. It had seemed likely.

Surely the three dudes in four-cornered hats had been behind the trouble stirred up between him and the aging ogre who had lived here. How many other houses were there along Bear Creek that would afford shelter to a city dude with two, maybe three, captive women?

Still he was filled with a strange sense of exhilaration that it took him some time to understand. Then he remembered Joe Spokane burying his nose in the bed. Miss Hallie was alive! Or at least, he soberly amended, she had been alive less than an hour ago. Sounds didn't travel for sour apples in this thick pine and tamarack woods but he knew that he would have heard a shot. Once more that drumming partridge tickled the edge of his hearing.

Then he was plunged once more into gloomy foreboding. As Mrs. Groby had scuttled out the front door with an infant and a patchwork quilt caught up in her arms there had been a single shot, a single sharp scream. Had somebody decided that it was time to make sure that Miss Hallie told no tales?

Dil stared upward into the snow clouds, wishing that he could pray as he had seen his mother pray in the long months when neither husband nor news had emerged from the Klondike. Instead he could feel only a choked anger. If he had not felt the need for silence he knew that he would have shouted it skyward: "You could've made any kind of world you wanted to. Why'd you have to go and make this kind?" It was a sin which Dil knew he would never find it in his heart to forgive, no matter how many sins his creator might forgive him.

Snow clouds flew past the moon, blotting it out most of the time. Each time the thin sliver of illumination was exposed for an instant Dil memorized another detail of the cabin and corral. Abruptly he knew what was wrong.

If Richardson was here, where were the horses and buckboard? Somewhere the partridge drummed again.

This time another rutting bird challenged it. Dil tried to remember if he had ever heard that sound at this time of year. It didn't seem right. He put his mouth to Joe Spokane's ear and asked about the horses.

The Indian shrugged.

"You think there's anybody inside there?" Dil insisted.

Spokane got his ear and asked, "Why don't you yell and find out?"

Dil guessed that it would have to be done sooner or later. "Richardson!" he yelled. "You comin' out or do I have to come in?"

The silence was absolute. Dil waited, listening. Nothing happened. He scuffled and found a pine cone. Wondering how many times this trick would work, he tossed it between the cabin and the corral. Still nothing happened.

Joe Spokane put his mouth to Dil's ear. "Please try not to shoot me," he murmured and disappeared into the shadows.

Dil waited, checking his background and hoping that he was invisible in the scrub. He opened the magazine of his rifle and made sure that it was fully loaded. Then he stepped to one side of where he had made the noise. Somewhere in the depths of the forest that fool partridge was drumming again.

"Dil!" It was Joe Spokane's voice. "Give our friend a shout."

Dil hesitated for a moment, then obliged.

"That, Mr. Richardson," Joe Spokane's voice came clearly from behind the cabin, "is merely to assure you that we are not involved in chicanery. You are faced with clear-cut alternatives: You may exit the front door of your humble refuge and surrender to the outraged citizenry of Bear Creek, who may or may not see fit to lynch you." There was a moment's hesitation. "Or you may effect an exit to the rear and fall into the hands of my tribesmen, who have their own time-honored methods of dealing with interlopers. And be assured we will not cavil at applying extreme measures." Suddenly behind the cabin there was a droning like an overturned beehive. The sound seemed to come from everywhere and nowhere, rising in volume until Dil could hardly believe it. He felt his hackles rise at the knowledge that somehow the whole damned tribe must have used ropes to lower itself down the gorge above the lean-to.

The droning, buzzing sound continued, gradually rising until it ended abruptly with a sharp yap like that of a rutting fox. After an instant it began again.

Even though he knew they were on his side Dil found the sound unnerving as it rebounded through the darkness, without source, untraceable, seeming to issue from behind every bush and tree. The droning buzz crescendoed again, ending in that short, barking yap, and silence prevailed. He tried to quiet his breathing. If it was frightening to him, what must it be to the city dude penned up in the house with a passel of women?

"You there, in the house!" he yelled. "Come on out this way and I'll try'n get you safe in to town." He waited for a moment, then added, "You go lightin' a shuck out the back way, you're gonna lose your hair sure as hell!"

Still there was silence inside the house. Dil wondered. The horses and buckboard were not here. Then he realized that that really didn't mean anything. Richardson must have grabbed Miss Hallie and lit out the instant he heard Dil's shot plow into Groby. He might have run, dragging the girl all the way here to Jake Nelson's cabin. And Mrs. Groby, leaving minutes later with her child, had probably found the buckboard and lit out for Winville to alert the law. But what had happened to Miz Haines? Was she dead somewhere in the shadows of Groby's yard? Or did Richardson have her here with him?

Once more that droning buzz began, coming from all sides, rising sharply, then ending with an abrupt yap. Dil felt hair rise on the nape of his neck. It was like the summer bees had made their home in the walls of the house which rising taxes had stolen from his widowed mother. Only the bees had buzzed constantly, so loudly that conversation was difficult, but never rising abruptly and terminating with this foxy yap. He knew that the sound was coming from Joe Spokane's friends, that they were his friends too. Yet there was something about the sound that opened some hitherto sealed part of his brain, releasing all the childhood terrors that had filled the darkened corners of his bedroom.

And still there was no sound from inside the cabin. Nobody there, he told himself. Then he was inspired. "Chief!" he yelled, "Blood brother, you got the fire arrows ready? We gotta burn him out."

"Soon," Spokane's voice came back through the darkness. "Soon we burn him." There was a low-pitched, chuckling laugh that rose slowly, playing an ascending chromatic scale of madness. Dil wondered if this was the pepper-and-salt-suited bureaucrat he was hearing.

"This is your last chance, Richardson," he yelled. "I ain't got a thing to lose anymore and I think it'll be fun t'sit out here and listen to you sizzle."

"You got something to lose all right!" It was a voice from Jake Nelson's cabin—the same voice that had been berating Groby.

"You got people on all sides of you," Dil called back. "If you don't want to send them women out first then me'n my people just gonna back off half a mile and let the Indians handle it."

On cue Joe Spokane emitted a bloodcurdling war whoop. An instant later that same droning buzz crescendoed.

"All right!" Richardson called, "I'm coming out. Don't shoot."

Dil aimed his rifle at the cabin, straining his eyes into the blackness, praying to unknown gods that he might repeat his luck with Groby. He couldn't see anything. He hoped he was equally invisible to the man inside Jake Nelson's cabin. Finally he saw something move. Belatedly he remembered to cock his rifle.

Richardson heard the click. "I have my hands straight up!" he shouted. "Please don't shoot."

"Where're the women?"

"Inside." Richardson moved unsurely in the blackness. The clouds parted for an instant and Dil could see that he was telling the truth. At least the mine manager's hands were over his head. He wondered if the man was armed. Richardson was moving at an angle and Dil realized that the man did not know exactly where he was.

Finally the man had moved far enough from the shadow to make retreat impractical. "Just keep your hands up and turn around," Dil called. When Richardson complied he began moving forward, rifle at ready. He hoped that Joe Spokane would show up in time to search the man. But Joe didn't. Dil dithered behind the manager, rifle in hand, knowing that it would be dangerous to put it down long enough to bind the other. Finally he saw the obvious solution to his problem. Lowering the hammer carefully, he lowered the octagonal rifle barrel with equal care across Richardson's head. The hollow pumpkin sound was most satisfying.

Richardson crumpled. Dil waited for a moment to see if he was going to move again. When he didn't Dil removed his belt and cinched it around Richardson's ankles. He searched for shoe laces but the manager was wearing laceless engineer's boots. He tore a sleeve off the man's shirt and ripped it into strips. He was just finishing tying the man's hands behind him when Joe Spokane appeared from nowhere.

"How many people you got with you?" Dil asked.

Spokane laughed.

"How'd they know where to find us?" Dil insisted. He put a finishing touch to Richardson's bonds, then went toward the cabin. "Got a match?"

The Indian didn't.

"Hasn't anybody out there got a match?"

Spokane laughed again. "It's the trees and the canyon face," he explained. "All kinds of echoes and diffusion."

Dil rushed into the darkened cabin and began fumbling toward where he remembered having seen the stove. There had to be a matchbox somewhere. "Hallie?" he called. "Miss Hallie, you in here?"

If she was, Miss Hallie wasn't saying.

Fighting down a rising sense of panic, Dil scrabbled about for the matchbox he knew had to be there somewhere. For the first time in his life he wished that he smoked. At least he would have had a match with him. With half his mind he tried to understand what the Indian was saying. "A whole goddamn tribe of Indians and nobody can come up with a match?" he snarled. He ran his hands over the wall, over the splintery shelf below the window. Where did Jake Nelson keep his goddamn matches?

"No whole tribe, goddamned or otherwise," Joe Spokane was saying with patient good humor. "Ah yes!"

Suddenly there was light and Dil realized that the Indian had finally found the matches. His eyes darted around the tiny cabin, looking for Miss Hallie. Finally he saw her and her mother, half buried beneath the stinking pile of blankets that had been Jake Nelson's bed. He pulled the blankets off of them. Both women were bound and gagged. He was trying to untie Miss Hallie when the match went out.

Agonizing centuries passed before the Indian lit another match and then a stub of candle. Dil wondered what he was doing dithering around with knots. He got out his jackknife and cut loose Miss Hallie, then Miz Haines. "What happened to you?" he asked the older woman. "Where were you when I needed you?"

"And where were *you* when I needed you?" Hallie asked in a voice shrill and grating from lack of use.

Dil looked around the cabin for water. There was none. He left Joe to tend the women and went outside to see what deviltry Richardson was cooking up. The mine manager was still unconscious. Dil wondered worriedly if he had hit too hard. He checked the man's bonds and made sure that he was not shamming. Then he went inside, where Joe Spokane was soft-soaping the two women, basking in their adulation just as if he had done it all alone.

Spokane glanced at Dil and grinned. "No tribe," he said and pointed at a funnel of rolled bark. He put the funnel to his mouth and, moving his free fist in and out of it like a mute, gave vent to that slow-rising crescendo of a buzz, ending with a sharp, foxy yap. Even seeing the Indian do it Dil felt his hackles rise. At least it explained how they had all just happened to be at the right spot at the right time. They hadn't.

CHAPTER 19

Miss Hallie seemed so ungrateful that Dil wondered momentarily if he had made a mistake in rescuing her. He saw a bucket in the corner of the cabin and escaped with it to the creek. When he came back she seemed less ferocious. Jake Nelson had never shaved and had no need of a mirror. Miss Hallie and Miz Haines cleaned each other up as best they could. "Can't you do something besides just stand there and watch?" Hallie snapped.

Dil sighed and went outside. Couldn't anything ever work out right? Girls were supposed to throw their arms around their rescuers and kiss them and sigh things like "my hero." If he'd known that she was going to be this prickly he wouldn't have bothered. And why, he wondered, did Joe Spokane have to be so vastly amused by it all?

"I believe we're now about to face a problem in logistics," the Indian said.

Dil was tired of trying to figure out what this kind of double talk meant but while he was trying to think up something crushing Spokane added, "We have two women in not the best of shape and a man who may not regain consciousness. How are we going to get them in to town before we all freeze?"

The clouds meant snow. And it was a most godawful walk in to town from Jake Nelson's place. "Maybe we can just send the women home to the Haines place," Dil hazarded. He stuck his head in the doorway of the frigid cabin, where Hallie and Miz Haines struggled to make each other presentable. Despite her ordeal and a total lack of facilities Dil found Miss Hallie disconcertingly presentable already. He wondered if all girls had this ability. She seemed less snappish now than when he had first uncovered her disheveled form beneath the pile of stinking blankets.

Miz Haines looked at him. "Didn't have a chance," she said. "Your Mr. Richardson come tearing out of the house like a wild bull." She fingered a red and swollen jawline. "Don't think he even saw me," she explained. "But he was all over me before I could even cock a pistol."

Dil considered this information. "Did he have Miss Hallie with him?"

Hallie nodded and in that same rusty-gate voice said, "They were jawin' back and forth and then I heard a shot and next thing he come runnin' out on the screen porch and slung me over his shoulder and lit out. He dropped me when he stumbled over Maw but I was still tied up."

"Didn't anybody shoot?"

Both women shook their heads.

Mystified, Dil left them to their toilette and stepped outside where Joe Spokane was examining Richardson. The mine superintendent was moaning and starting to squirm. "Think we can walk him in to town?" Dil asked.

Spokane grinned. "I couldn't say. It might be amusing to try."

Dil stared down at the moaning man, reflecting on all the misery he had caused—and all just to add two cents to the value of several thousand pieces of paper. "It ain't right," he grumbled. "No man ought to have that much power."

"Careful," Spokane warned. "Your opinions come dangerously close to subversion."

Finally they were all on their feet, a mournful little

caravan marching the weary miles back toward Winville. Dil wondered why he felt so deflated. It was over. He had gotten Miss Hallie back alive. He had caught the villain—done everything he had set out to do. Why wasn't he jumping up and down and kicking his heels?

Suddenly Joe Spokane stopped prodding Richardson along in front of them. "Perhaps we won't have to walk all the way after all," he murmured. A moment later Dil heard it too.

Within a minute they could hear the sound of several automobiles struggling up the collection of ruts the county chose to call the Bear Creek road. Soon there was an occasional flash of headlight in the trees. "I suppose you'll realize who got in to town and spread the alarm," Spokane said soberly.

Dil had been thinking on it for several minutes now. Mrs. Groby! She had taken the buckboard and old Bill, with the other nameless city dude Dil had shot still on his broad back. And the lot she had stirred up would be loaded for bear. More specifically, loaded for Dil. "Better get them off in the brush," he muttered.

Spokane stared at him in the sudden illumination from a rift in snow clouds. "You're going to stand out in the middle of the road and get shot?"

"Not if I can help it," Dil said. "But while they're jawin' with me maybe you can take Richardson and the ladies past 'em somehow through the brush and get in to town."

"Where in town?"

It was a good question. The sheriff was dead. The deputy was a wholly owned and operated subsidiary of the mining company. There had to be some legal means of re-establishing law and order in this county. But Dil didn't know how to begin.

The problem was unexpectedly resolved when Miss

Hallie snapped, "If you think I'm gonna go hide in the brush you got another think a-comin'!" They were still wrangling in the middle of the road when the headlights of the first automobile outlined them.

And suddenly they were surrounded by armed men. It didn't work out at all the way Dil and Joe Spokane had expected. Miss Hallie's shrill voice and Miz Haines' corroboration had abruptly put Dil and Joe Spokane on the side of the angels. A burly Bear Creeker was tossing a lariat repeatedly, trying to get the loose end over a spruce limb. But it was for the mine manager.

"No!" Dil said abruptly. "You ain't gonna lynch Richardson."

Immediately he sensed his newly won popularity starting to decline. "Why not?" a surly voice asked. "He was willing to kill all of us."

"Because if we lynch him, they'll just send in an army or national guard or whatever it is the mine owners use when they want to steal some homesteader's land."

The Bear Creekers had come out here in the middle of the night to hang somebody. They were not in a mood for disappointment. The burly man was still trying to get his rope end over a spruce limb.

"They always do things nice and legal," Dil yelled over the strident voices. "So we better do things legal too. We got plenty of proof to give Richardson a trial and then hang him."

"In this county, with this sheriff?" It was a sarcastic question.

Abruptly Joe Spokane contributed. "Mr. Reeves is right," he said. "But there's probably nothing wrong in expressing a little displeasure with your deputy's biased attitude. If properly approached, perhaps he could be induced to resign and Mr. Reeves could by unanimous acclaim serve as county sheriff pending a special election."

Dil was stunned. "Is that legal?" he asked.

"Probably not," Spokane grinned. "But possession is nine points of the law and by election time it might be difficult for a mining company manager on trial for his life to exorcise a popular hero."

"I dunno if I want to be sheriff," Dil said.

Spokane indicated the mob of Bear Creekers who had just as suddenly swung back to enthusiastic acceptance of Dil. "You want to cross them again?" he murmured.

Dil guessed that out here, umpteen miles from town, with it getting ready to snow, was no place to quibble. There was backing and filling and groups of burly men pushing vehicles out of the mud until finally they were all turned around and headed back toward Winville. Dil and a mute, defeated Richardson rode in the lead car, a Star with the top up but no side curtains. Distributed behind them in other cars were Joe Spokane and the Haines women.

Sitting with the 45-90 between his knees, he bounced along the ruts, wondering what would happen when they reached the sheriff's office in Winville. He began shivering. It began to snow lightly but he guessed that if it got no worse the automobiles would make it back to town without mishap. They were passing the ford where Nellie's carcass still flung legs defiantly skyward when he roused from his chill reverie to realize that it was dawning.

The sheriff's office was dark and empty when they drove down the main street. Dil wondered where the deputy lived. He didn't even know the man's name. There was a moment of conference with the man who drove the lead car, then they proceeded down the street toward the opulence of the James J. Hill Hotel. The night clerk was awake, alerted by the sound of a half-dozen automobiles banging and popping in the street before his building.

Carrying his rifle casually, Dil entered the lobby. "You know where the deputy is?" he asked. "We got a prisoner."

The deputy didn't live at the hotel but he lived in a boarding house half a block down the street. Dil pounded on the door until an outraged woman in a lace nightcap peered from an upper-story window. Finally she came downstairs and opened the door. Dil conferred with her briefly and then he was in a small upstairs room where the young man who had been settling so comfortably into the sheriff's office was now having somewhat more difficulty in finding the legs of his trousers.

"I got Richardson dead to rights down there," Dil said flatly. "Murder, kidnapping, you name it."

The deputy stared, at a loss for a way to handle this situation. Dil guessed that it was time to help him make up his mind. "I got close to a hundred Bear Creekers out there too. They're pretty fed up with the way the law couldn't do anything and how I had to go out and rescue that girl myself." He looked down on the deputy, who was still struggling to get his pants on. "I stopped 'em from lynching Richardson but they're still hankerin' to hang somebody. You want to come down and explain why you couldn't do anything back when we needed help—before we all got our guns loaded and ready?"

The deputy did not find the prospect attractive.

"You're still alive," Dil said. "And so far you ain't wearin' any tar or feathers. Maybe you want to quit lawin' for this county?"

The deputy guessed that he did.

"And maybe since there ain't no other lawman and the sheriff promised me the job, you might's well hand over the badge and your guns and the keys to the jail and all that?"

The deputy stared at the nearly half-inch-wide hole in the end of Dil's 45-90 and decided that these demands were not unreasonable. After some further struggle he finally got his pants on. They were on backward but he guessed that that was good enough. Moments later the deputy was lighting a shuck out the back door of the boarding house, heading for less hostile climes.

So that was that and with a bewildering suddenness Dil found himself de facto sheriff and heir apparent, unless the mining interests could halt their disarrayed retreat and put up some straw man against the wave of popularity that was standing him drinks, buying him cigars, making free with all the little niceties he could have used a week ago. Now that he was on top, friends and supporters were crawling from beneath every flat rock in the county.

It took him a day to discover that Mrs. Groby had not been all that keen on her husband's role, that she had stopped at Joe Hagen's place instead of in town, and had probably contributed more than anyone else to his sudden success. Miz Haines had made her peace with Mrs. Groby. Dil supposed there were reasons for arresting her but, not possessing a legal mind, he was ready to call it quits. He had done her some injury too—made her a widow whether she welcomed it or not. He studiously avoided coming face to face with the woman and she had the good sense to stay out of his way.

Which left only the problem of prosecuting Richardson, or rather of making sure that the county's suddenly ownerless legal apparatus sensed the winds of change and weathercocked promptly. The district attorney had not been overly impressed by Dil and his rifle but he had a proper regard for the Bear Creekers' voting power. And the local newspaper had also caught a whiff of the heady air of freedom now that the mining interests were in retreat. There was talk of a federal investigation and clippings of stories in Washington newspapers where Mr. Wilson just about had to take notice of what was happening to the conservation program he had inherited from Roosevelt and Taft—providing he ever got a moment free from his ongoing task of keeping America out of war.

Like a good fairy or a bad politician, Joe Spokane had disappeared while Dil was confronting a deputy who couldn't get his pants on properly with both hands. In the week since then Dil had bungled about, learning his way into the office of sheriff, handling details like the burial of the man he had shot, of seeing that old Bill was properly fed and oated at the livery stable.

It had taken him another day to discover that the dead sheriff's Ford roadster was back in this end of the county, that it went with the job and had not belonged to the scholarly little man, and that if he was going to cover this county properly he had better learn how to drive it.

That took most of another forenoon. Finally he had bounced and jerked the rutted miles out to the Haines place to call on Miss Hallie.

CHAPTER 20

Miz Haines was boiling clothes out in the yard when he arrived. "How's lawin'?" she asked.

Dil shrugged. "Guess a man can get used to anything in time. How's Miss Hallie?"

"Out chasin' down a cow."

"You been havin' more trouble?" Dil asked sharply.

Miz Haines shook her head. "Just a fence-jumpin' cow. Al was goin' to beef her soon's we raised another heifer."

At the mention of Al Haines they both grew silent. Finally Dil asked, "You two gonna make it all right out here without a man?"

"Won't be easy," Miz Haines said. "But leastways there's two of *us*."

For a moment Dil didn't see what she was getting at. Then he remembered Mrs. Groby alone on a farmstead very like this, with no company but a yearling child. Abruptly he recalled something his mother had said once after Papa had failed to come home from the Klondike. "A man," he said musingly, "needs a woman if he's going to get along. But a woman's all right as long's she got a young'un."

Miz Haines gave him a sharp look. "You got no call tellin' me that," she snapped.

At that moment Miss Hallie, in bib overalls, rode into the yard, leading a cow. Miz Haines disappeared inside the house.

Later it was to occur to Dil that he knew the words but

he didn't know the tune. Miss Hallie wasn't much help either. Goldang, he thought. After all the trouble he'd gone to you'd think she could at least be neighborly! Instead she was asking, "Don't you know enough to give a lady fair warning? Now you just sit yourself down there by the waterin' trough and give me time to go get some clothes on!"

She had seemed anything but naked to Dil, decked out in oversized flannel shirt and bib overalls. He wondered if he would ever understand what went on inside a woman's mind. Suddenly he realized what Miz Haines had been trying to tell him: that he had no woman and Miss Hallie had no young'un. Why couldn't she say things straight out? Goldanged women were worse than Joe Spokane. He was wondering what had happened to the bureaucratic-tongued Indian when Miss Hallie finally reappeared in the kitchen doorway.

This time she wore something which Dil would, about the time it was going out of style, learn was called sprigged muslin. He would never have been able to describe it except that with yards of it billowing around Miss Hallie she looked very different from the way she looked in bib overalls. She even talked differently. "Well, Mr. Reeves," she asked, "what tears you from your duties in Winville?"

"Don't rightly know," Dil said and dug the toe of his new boots into the damp soil of the barnyard. There was an awkward silence. He gazed entreatingly at Miss Hallie but she was fortified behind yards of muslin. Abruptly he gave up. "Guess I better get on back in to town," he mumbled and tried to remember where to set the spark and gas levers before cranking the flivver.

"Dil! Where you goin'?"

"Where you want me to go?"

"Well, you come all the way out here for somethin', didn't you?"

Dil straightened up from his first abortive attempt to crank the flivver. "Yeah," he admitted.

"Well, what was it?"

Desperately he improvised some way out of this predicament. "Uh—that night it all happened, uh—when Mrs. Groby and her young'un lit out the door I heard a shot and somebody screamed. You got any idea who done it?"

Miss Hallie seemed annoyed. "She dropped one of her husband's pistols and it went off," she snapped.

"Oh." There was another long silence. "Well—I got to be goin'." Once more he bent to crank the flivver.

"You drove all the way out here to ask me that?"

"Well, no," Dil admitted. "I, uh—I come out to ask if you could cook."

"Yes!" Hallie snapped. "I can cook and boil clothes and chase cows and milk them and feed chickens and gather eggs, and—and I'm goldanged sick of it all!" Suddenly Miss Hallie seemed very close to tears.

"Yeah, uh, well—I got to be goin'."

"Go on back to town!" Hallie shrieked. "Git!"

"Goldang it, I didn't come out here just to get yelled at!"

"Then why did you come out?"

"Well, I, I was kind of thinkin' about gettin' married."

There! He'd said it. And having said it he was very sure that he didn't really want to get married at all, but suddenly Hallie was all over him and there just didn't seem to be any way to get out of it now, and the first thing Dil knew he was standing beside Miss Hallie in town, wearing a stiff collar that was digging into his neck, and goldang it, how did he ever get into this anyhow?

Next day in the sheriff's office Joe Spokane was gravely amused but he hadn't the slightest idea how Dil had gotten into it either. "Something to do with the ductless glands, I believe," the Indian said. "But usually they're more active around April than in late October. By the way, did you know Richardson's attorneys have petitioned for a change of venue?"

"What's that mean?"

"Means they're trying to get him tried in a different county where they can pack the jury and there won't be any Bear Creekers on it."

"You suppose he'll get off?"

The Indian shrugged. "Even a change of venue can't do away with witnesses. Just stick to the truth and no attorney can make a fool of you when you're on the stand."

Dil thought for a moment and decided that this was sound advice. "You think we got them hydraulickers licked?" he finally asked.

"No."

"No? After all the hell we went through?"

The Indian sighed. "You'll get lazy. People forget. First thing you know somebody's going to introduce a harmless little piece of legislation that doesn't really mean anything to anyone. Somebody may wonder about it but they'll let it pass."

Dil stared at him.

"Then, somebody else's going to petition for an easement or some such thing—all perfectly legal and proper and nobody's going to pay the slightest bit of attention until someday three or five or maybe ten years from now everybody in lower Bear Creek wakes up neck deep in hydraulicker's mud." Spokane paused for a moment. "By the way, how goes the special election? Are you going to be the new sheriff?"

"Filing time's past," Dil said. "Nobody's running against me."

"Oh?" Spokane seemed genuinely surprised. "So that's how they're going to do it," he mused.

"Do what?" Dil asked. "What can I do to keep them hydraulickers from cuttin' up Bear Creek?"

"That's difficult to predict," Spokane said. "Some paleface president of yours once remarked that eternal vigilance is the price of liberty."

Dil sighed and tried to understand what Spokane was saying. "Come on," he said. "I'll buy you some lunch."

"Thanks," Spokane said. "But the only food fit to eat in this town is in the Jim Hill and unfortunately, in this land of the free, Indians and liquor licenses are incompatible." He punched Dil on the shoulder. "Keep up the good fight," he admonished. "I'll be seeing you."

"Yeah," Dil said thoughtfully. He locked up the office and began strolling toward the hotel. Once the county got its accounting straightened out and started paying him regularly he intended to get a decent house in town so that he wouldn't have to drive clear out Bear Creek every night to the Haines house, where Hallie and his mother-in-law waited. It was going to have to be soon, he knew, for before long the snow would be too deep for the flivver to make it.

He was just sitting down to eat his solitary lunch when a dapper man with a briefcase approached him. "Mr. Reeves?"

Dil nodded.

"May I have a word with you?"

"Guess so," Dil said and kicked out a chair.

"My clients feel you have been sorely wronged," the dapper man said once he had made himself comfortable. "I have been charged with making suitable restitution."

Dil sighed and guessed that now that he was going to be sheriff he was going to have to learn to understand that kind of talk. He waited for the dapper man to continue. Sooner or later these smooth-talking men always slipped back into plain English long enough for him to guess what it was all about.

"Due to the misplaced zeal of certain individuals you have been inconvenienced in various ways. Though responsibility can in no way be acknowledged or assigned for these torts, it is my clients' feeling that justice may best be served by rendering a prompt gratuity."

Dil stared at the dapper little man, waiting for him to lapse into plain English. The stranger seemed uncomfortable under Dil's steady stare.

"May I take it that you would not be averse to such an arrangement?"

Sooner or later this stranger was going to get to the point. Dil stared while the Jim Hill's waiter put a plate of liver and onions on the table. When the other man failed to elucidate he began eating.

"Uh—perhaps once you've seen the tender . . ." The small man fiddled with his briefcase and removed a large manila envelope. When Dil started to open it he hastily added, "Perhaps in some less conspicuous place—"

Dil tore open the envelope. Inside was a sizable bundle of gold and silver certificates. He had never seen that much money in his life. Across the dining room the waiter was suddenly busy rearranging crockery. "How much is in there?" Dil asked.

"Five thousand dollars."

Dil did mental sums. That was about three years' pay for lawin'. "What's it for?"

"Restitution. My clients feel you've been ill used and they wish to make amends."

"Somebody's tryin' to buy a handshake?" Dil's voice had become imperceptibly louder.

"Certainly not!" The little man was indignant.

"Then what's it for? Tell me simple, without any turtles or institutions."

"My clients are sorry. This is their way of apologizing."

"For what?"

"For the various wrongs and inconveniences you've suffered."

"Oh? They done it to me? Who *are* they?" The clatter at neighboring tables was abruptly stilled.

The stranger ran a finger around his collar. "My clients disclaim responsibility for any acts and wish to emphasize that this is a voluntary gift and in no sense implies any legal claim past or future."

Dil thought for a moment. "This is for gettin' shot at, my horse dead, my wife kidnapped, and Al Haines killed?"

"Of course not," the stranger hastened. "But with the county's lax fiscal policy and your new expenses my clients thought it might be a friendly gesture." He paused and wiped his forehead. "Call it a campaign contribution. Surely you'll have expenses."

"Ain't nobody runnin' against me."

"Ummm, yes, well . . ."

Dil wondered if he was slow-witted or just inexperienced. Looking at the dapper little man who was offering him money, he saw another dimension in the problem. The county was apologetic as all get-out but so far he hadn't actually received any salary. Bills were piling up and lately Hallie had been dropping ominous hints about a layette, whatever that was. He wondered if it always started this way.

The dead sheriff must have been young once. Maybe he'd had problems too. He must have been grateful for a little help offered with no strings attached. It might be years before a man discovered how tightly the strings were attached—when he found himself breaking a strike or evicting a widow while making pious noises about law and order.

"Mr. Jenkins," he said, "have you been handin' out

money to the Indians or any of the Bear Creekers that starved when your bank wouldn't see them through? Seems t'me even Jake Nelson and Groby got done dirty by your owners. You done anything for Mrs. Groby?"

"Well, uh, not yet, but we have plans—"

"Sure you do. But I'm the one can hurt you so I'm the one you have to buy."

"Really, Mr. Reeves, these allegations are most irregular. My clients are offering a campaign contribution out of their own free will.

"Yup," Dil said. "Ain't nothin' like free will." He paused with a forkful of liver and onions halfway to his mouth. "Mr. Jenkins, you just sit there nice and quiet whilst I finish eatin' and then I'll have a message for your owners."

"I'm afraid my clients need a clear-cut statement of intent. And really, I have other errands to complete this afternoon."

Dil eyed the little man. "All right, Mr. Jenkins," he sighed. "You're under arrest. Is that clear enough?"

The dapper little man was aghast as Dil frogwalked him out of the dining room. "You can't arrest me!" he protested.

"Maybe not. But I can put you in jail." He walked the sputtering little man down the street, leaving his liver and onions to cool. He supposed the stranger could produce a dozen different bits of paper to get himself out of jail before nightfall. That wasn't what really worried Dil. He was looking ahead to the years when his family would be bigger, his salary smaller. As long as he was sheriff the little men with bags full of money would keep coming.

He wondered how long he could keep faith with the citizens of Bear Creek.